SOMEONE HAS TO DIE

A Lenny Moss Mystery

By Timothy Sheard

HARDBALL

PRESS

THE REVIEWERS PRAISE LENNY MOSS!

This Won't Hurt A Bit

"Things get off to a macabre start...when a student at a Philadelphia teaching hospital identifies the cadaver she is dissecting in anatomy class as a medical resident she once slept with. Although hospital administrators are relieved when a troublesome laundry worker is charged with the murder, outraged staff members go to their union representative, a scrappy custodian named Lenny Moss, and ask him to find the real killer. Since there's no merit to the case against the laundry worker to begin with, Lenny is just wasting his time. But Sheard, a veteran nurse, makes sure that readers do not waste theirs. His intimate view of Lenny's world is a gentle eyeopener into the way a large institution looks from a workingman's perspective."
New York Times

Some Cuts Never Heal

"This well-plotted page-turner is guaranteed to scare the bejesus out of anyone anticipating a hospital stay anytime in the near future." **Publishers Weekly**

"Sheard provides...polished prose and elements of warmth and humor. Strongly recommended for most mystery collections."
Library Journal

"If your pulse quickens for ER on Thursday nights, you'll want a dose of Timothy Sheard's medicine ... The well-meaning, hard-working hospital folks will warm your heart, while the cold realities of modern medical care will raise your blood pressure and keep you turning the pages." **Rocky Mountain News**

A Race Against Death

"While most shop stewards do not get involved in murder mysteries, they solve tough problems at work every day. Now they can look up to a fictional role model—Super Steward Lenny Moss." **Public Employee Press** Review

"Timothy Sheard provides a delightful hospital investigative tale that grips readers from the moment that Dr. Singh and his team apply CPR, but fail." **Mysteries Galore**

Slim To None

"Here's a page flipper, a murder mystery set in a hospital where the invisible, everyday workers are the key...Their practical knowledge, solidarity and smarts solve this confusing case that leads us down all sorts of blind paths with lives on the line...a great read, a complicated mystery, good friends, comradeship in hard times, and union workers shown in full humanity. Get it now!" **Earl Silbar, AFSCME 3506, City Colleges of Chicago**

No Place To Be Sick

"Does such a wonderful job of showing workers uniting to fight for justice that...unions have used Sheard's books for steward training. Find out if Lenny & his friends win their battle in this roller coaster of a story." **Union Communications**

"There's enough suspense, fear and chills running up and down your spine to make you keep on reading it in one fell swoop. Watch your back if you're alone in the house!" **Pride & A Paycheck**

Published by Hard Ball Press.
Information available at: www.hardballpress.com
ISBN: 978-0-9862400-6-5

Cover art by Patty Henderson
www.boulevardphotografica.yolasite.com.

Exterior and interior book design by D. Bass

Library of Congress Cataloging-in-Publication Data
Sheard, Timothy
Someone Has To Die: A Lenny Moss Mystery/Timothy Sheard
1. Philadelphia (PA) 2. Hospitals. 3. Lenny Moss.

For Paula

Remember when we were children
The afternoon seemed endless
We'd play in the street 'til our mother called us home…
—Chris Sheard

Lenny Moss grasped the bars of the jail cell and cursed his fate.

"Jesus H. Christ, this is the most fucked up situation I've been in since the time we got arrested at that anti-Klan demonstration down in Delaware."

Moose Maddox chuckled, recalling the turbulent day. "Heh, heh. 'Member that skinny girl, she ran between the cops on horseback and pulled the hood off o' the lead klansman?"

"That was so sweet!" said Lenny. "She kept punching the bastard in the nose 'til a cop grabbed her by the hair and dragged her away."

"We spent a night and a day in that little town jail," said Moose. "You wasn't complaining then."

"Yeah, well, I was a lot younger and stupider. And the Delaware jail food was a lot better." Lenny looked out through the bars at the empty hallway. "Tell me again, Moose, how the hell did I end up in a jail cell with my best friend?"

"No mystery, you stood up and did the right thing, like you always do. Problem is, the boss did what he always do, so here we are."

"We shouldn't be arrested for carrying out our union duties. Written up, okay. Fired, even, sure, but not arrested and facing felony charges."

"Yeah we were doin' union stuff, but that's not what landed us in jail. It was how we was doin' it."

Lenny grumbled. He thought Moose was exaggerating how much they had stepped over the line of protected union activity. But hey, the bosses broke the law every day, sometimes you've got to stretch the boundaries; take some chances; live a little bit outside the law. Lenny well knew the trick was not getting caught.

And having a good lawyer.

Moose clapped his friend on the shoulder with a big hand. "We'll make bail and be out b'fore the sun comes up, don't you worry."

"I don't worry about getting out, I worry about keeping my job. And you keeping yours, the hospital is gonna try to use this arrest against us, you know that's what they'll do."

"O' course they're gonna use it, they ain't stupid. But we're smarter than they are, Lenny, we'll beat 'em at their own game."

"Really? Tell me how you plan to do that."

"Don't worry, I'm workin' on it."

Lenny worried about it. Then he had a gloomy thought.

"Moose, your time in jail way back when, I hope that's not gonna keep you from making bail."

"Nah, that was a juvey charge. It's been, what do you call it, erased..."

"Expunged?"

"Yeah, expunged. Don't worry, you'll be back home with Patience and the kids by breakfast time."

"I hope so. When I'm not around, Patience tries to feed Malcolm that healthy vegetarian crap. He's gonna miss my French toast cooked in bacon fat and covered with syrup."

"Cut it out, you're makin' me hungry."

"Sorry."

Lenny wrapped his hands around the bars once more. "I don't even have a tin cup to rattle, all I've got is fricking styrofoam! The noise it makes is pathetic."

Moose joined Lenny to stand at the bars. He knew his friend sometimes sank into one of his dark moods. But somehow he always came out of the gloom and led the charge, fighting the good fight.

The two men stared through the bars at the bare wall across the hall and waited.

And remembered...

Anna Louisa pushed her rolling medication cart to the next room, the light of the computer screen illuminating her café con leche face. A new hire with less than a year seniority stuck on the graveyard shift, the young nurse was still not used to working through the long night. By six in the morning the grind of the twelve hour shift had made her mind numb and fuzzy.

The nurse called up the medication profile for Mrs. Gershawn in 705, who was due to receive an antibiotic at 6 am. Removing the small intravenous bag from the drawer, she stepped silently into the room, turned on the over-bed light and checked the patient's ID band on her wrist, then she hung the medication on the IV pole.

Awakened by the nurse's ministrations, Mrs. Gershawn opened her eyes and mumbled in a sleepy voice, "Is breakfast here yet?"

"Sorry to wake you, Missus Gershawn," the nurse whispered, "it's Anna Louisa with your medication."

The nurse checked the name of the drug and the dosage one more time before opening the roller clamp and letting the drug drip, drip into the patient's vein. Not long out of her probationary period, she didn't want any medication errors on her record, there were too many new grads all clamoring for a job at James Madison Hospital.

"Try to get back to sleep, ma'am," Anna Louisa said, putting out the light. "Breakfast won't be up for hours."

As the grumbling Mrs. Gershawn closed her eyes and

settled back into the bed, the nurse hurried to complete her last rounds. Since the patient next door in 706 was not due any meds until the day shift began, Anna merely peeked in to check that Mr. Landry was sleeping soundly. Casting her flashlight on the A bed, she watched the slow rise and fall of his chest and saw that the IV pump was maintaining a slow continuous infusion. The B-bed was empty, a small miracle that she had escaped a new admission all night, so the nurse didn't have to go into the room to look around the drawn curtain at the bed by the window.

She pushed her cart on to the next room, her feet aching and her eyes heavy, hoping to get all her meds passed within the dreaded thirty-minute grace period. Check off a med more than thirty minutes after it was due to be given, or, worst of all, fail to administer a drug without a computer-approved exception, and it meant another morning staying late to explain to the head nurse why she was such a slow, stupid excuse for a nurse.

Maddy, the nurse's aide working with Anna Louisa, poked her head out from a room across the hall and asked for help changing a patient. "This guy's two hundred pounds of dead weight, girl, I've got to have some help turning him, I can't do his back and change the wet sheets all by my lonesome."

Anna Louisa stared for a few seconds at her computer screen. Did she have time to help Maddy and still get her last meds out on time? It would be close, but how could she not help her co-worker, Maddy was a saint who never complained when asked to make a run for the nurse to the pharmacy or central stores.

"Okay, let's turn him and get him on dry sheets. I don't want the day shift complaining about any work I left for them."

<><><>

Pulling the straight razor down across his neck, Robert Reichart enjoyed the feel of the blade as it scraped his skin, slicing the hairs in a broad swipe. He wiped the shaving cream and the line of black hairs from the blade with a towel, then held the stainless steel blade once more poised over his neck.

How easy it would be to slice the carotid artery, he thought. My pumping heart would send gushers of bright, hot blood onto the mirror and into the sink.

Robert smiled at the thought of suicide. He wasn't really tempted to do it, his life was far too valuable to waste on a premature death. He had too much to do, managing a leading Philadelphia medical center and advancing the agenda of the Croesus Group; too many enemies to defeat. There were fires to put out, obstructionists to vanquish.

But should he ever hear one of his doctors give him a fatal diagnosis — cancer of the pancreas, or brain — he knew it would be infinitely preferable to end his life on his own terms, before he became a feeble, drooling idiot. Before he became incontinent and smelled of urine and shit.

Sartre had it right: every day we face a choice to live or to die. We are totally free to throw ourselves off a bridge, jump in front of a speeding train or truck, put the muzzle of a gun to our head...

He liked to think that, should he decide he'd had enough of life, that he had accomplished all he'd set out to do, he would not put the gun into his mouth in the traditional manner. Rather, he would point the gun directly at his right eye. He would look into the black hollow of the barrel and watch the flash as the gunpowder ignited. He would

7

hear the sharp retort of the explosion, and see the bullet come hurtling at him. A short blaze of pain, then silence. Emptiness. From being to nothingness, the final progression.

Perhaps one day, but not today.

Today he had mountains to climb; dragons to slay. Finishing his shave, Martin dressed in a fresh double breasted charcoal gray suit, then called for his car and his breakfast, leaving just enough time to arrive at the hospital before the day shift began so he could observe his troops assembling.

James Madison Medical Center was awaiting his strong hand at the tiller. He would keep the ship on its proper course and throw overboard the doubters and malingerers; especially those troublesome union agitators who stirred up the employees, beginning first and foremost with that annoying pest, Lenny Moss.

After taking report from the sleepy Anna Louisa, Mimi looked to see if the doctors on morning rounds had entered any STAT orders on her patients. The new computer system flagged STAT orders in red, so it only took a few seconds for her to scan her list on the computer screen and see that none of the new orders had the dreaded red flag. Muttering a prayer of thanks for small favors, she gathered up her equipment, stacked it on the rolling med cart, and started on her first rounds of the day.

In room 705 she saw that Mrs. Gershawn was awake. As Mimi pressed the control button to raise the head of the bed, the old woman greeted her with a toothy smile, her dentures having benefitted from a good soaking in a strong soapy solution during the night. "Is breakfast here yet?" asked Gershawn.

"I haven't seen the food cart yet, ma'am, but it should be here any minute."

The old lady's roommate, Miss Gittens, a slim, young-looking eighty year old, was already out of bed and in the bathroom washing up. When Mimi asked if the woman needed any assistance, the elderly woman called back that she was "hunky-dory, thank you very much, don't bother about me!"

Mimi scanned her work list. She saw that there were three complete bed baths and five partial baths to be done, along with two dressing changes, one of them that foul-smelling prostate cancer wound that always made her gag, and knew it was going to be a long morning.

The nurse approached room 706 to see if Mr. Landry was awake yet and how his back ache was progressing. He was scheduled for discharge later that day and should be able to wash up by himself in the bathroom.

Stepping into the room, the nurse saw that Landry was lying on his back with his mouth and eyes open. Odd. There was the rare patient who slept with his eyes open, but the open mouth looked all wrong.

She stepped to the bed and put a hand lightly on the patient's chest. There was no rise and fall. Growing alarmed, she felt at the wrist for a pulse. The skin was cold to the touch, the radial artery, pulseless. Double-checking for a pulse at the carotid artery in the neck, Mimi confirmed the patient was in cardiac and respiratory arrest.

"Dammit!" She rushed to the doorway and called out to the other nurse on duty, "Melba, we have a code in room seven-o-six! Bring the cart!"

After calling the operator on the portable communication device around her neck and requesting the code team,

Mimi prepared to administer mouth-to-mouth resuscitation, there being no bag-valve mask in the room. She put one hand beneath the patient's neck and tried to lift his torso up enough to remove the pillow beneath his head, but the patient's body was so stiff, she was unable to get him to bend at the waist.

"Holy shit!" she cried, realizing that rigor mortise had set in. She looked toward the B bed behind the drawn curtain, worrying she might have disturbed the roommate. But she remembered Anna Louisa had reported the B bed had remained empty all night.

Unable to pry open the dead man's mouth, she pinched his nose, pressed her mouth against his and blew in a lungful of air. Not that there was any hope of resuscitating Mr. Landry, his lips were ice cold. Mimi knew that rigor doesn't begin until three or four hours after death, which meant the poor man had been dead for at least the last three hours of the night shift.

Why hadn't Anna Louisa realized the patient was dead? She wasn't a new nurse fresh out of school. How could she miss that the patient had expired hours ago?

As the other nurse rushed into the room with the crash cart, smashing it into the footboard, Mimi told her to relax, there was no need to hurry. "Calm yourself down, Melba, this one's a slow code," she said. "The poor soul has been down for hours, there's no bringing this one back."

3

Lenny Moss ran his mop across the floor in room 706, enjoying the scent of lemon and bleach in the soapy water. He was a thickly built man, not very tall, with a large nose, black bushy eyebrows and a bald spot on the back of his head. His hands were thickly calloused and strong, his eyes often dark, sometimes gleeful, always wary.

The antiseptic solution he liked to use would kill the deadly bacteria that flourished in the hospital and posed such a grave risk to the patients. The dreaded Superbugs. Not that anyone gave his housekeeping department much credit for the drop in hospital acquired infections that the administration had reported this year with great fanfare. At least Dr. Auginello would say something positive about their work, the Infectious Disease doctor was one of the few who gave credit where credit was due for keeping the infection rate down.

Setting the yellow caution sign in the doorway, Lenny was pushing his bucket down to the next room when he saw Mimi at her rolling computer station looking even more miserable than usual.

"Hey, Mimi. I heard about your code this morning. Tough way to start your shift."

"Tell me about it. The team didn't work for more than like five minutes before the chief resident starting chewing me out for calling a code on a patient in full rigor. Like it was my fault."

"Those guys live in a dream."

"For real. Anyhow, I made out the code report, and I had to put down that I found the body already stiff, which means he must have died beaucoup hours before the end of the night shift."

"Huh. How come the night nurse didn't see he was dead?"

"That's the part that's got me so upset, Lenny. Anna Luisa is a real good nurse. Very meticulous. I know, I mentored her for a whole month when she came on staff last year. She's like a military style nurse, everything on time and double checked."

"A little O-C."

"She's very much O-C, which in a nurse is a good thing, it means we don't stray from the proper protocol, we do everything by the book." Mimi picked up some towels and a wash rag to help the aide with a bed bath. "I feel really really bad for Anna, they're going to fire her, no doubt in my mind. And you know Mother Burgess is gonna report her to the nursing licensing board. She'll never work in this profession again."

Mimi grabbed Lenny's arm and drew him closer. In a whisper she told him, "That's not the worst part. I'm afraid she might be in trouble with the law."

When Lenny gave her a quizzical look, the nurse added that the blood work drawn during the code was all out of whack. "The code team doctor said it looked to him like the patient died from a medication error. It makes no sense, Anna doesn't make mistakes like that. No way no how."

Lenny knew that a drug error resulting in a patient death could lead to a prosecution. As he watched Mimi go into the room across the hall to begin the bath, Lenny picked up his mop and moved on to the next room, feeling a familiar sense of gloom that a good hospital worker was going to get the shaft. Not that he could do anything about it, the nurse wasn't in his union. She wasn't in any union, for that matter.

Realizing there was no way that he could help a young woman he barely knew, having only seen her giving report and staying late to finish up her charting, Lenny turned his mind to the day's tasks. Would he have to deal with another exploding toilet? Or a broken soil pipe that rained urine down on some pissed off administrator's desk? More mouse droppings in the kitchen? The day was bound to be full of surprises and disgusting challenges.

He ran the mop over the old marble floor, finding solace in a familiar job and a familiar rhythm in the work, and trying to get into a positive frame of mind before the damned union meeting that afternoon. The contract negotiations with the new owners were going nowhere.

Gloria Green pulled a heavy bag of dirty laundry from the big basket beneath the laundry chute and hoisted it over her shoulder. A small, plump woman with short hair and bright eyes, she could haul laundry bags as well as any man, and with a good deal more humor. Gloria emptied the bag into one of the big industrial machines, careful not to squeeze the bag in case it contained a hidden needle or scalpel. She had suffered more than her share of puncture injuries over the years working in the laundry, thankfully never contracting hepatitis or HIV. One time she had found an evil looking, foot long needle among the sheets. When Infection Control came to investigate, they informed her it was used to puncture the spinal cord. How any doctor or medical student could leave that in the bed linen was beyond her understanding.

She wiped a bead of sweat from her brow and called out to her co-worker, "Yo, Evie, you goin' to the meeting after work today?"

"What meeting's that?" said Evie.

Gloria frowned and shook her head. "The union meeting. You saw the flyer in the locker room, didn't you? There's a meeting to talk about saving our benefits. It's at five o'clock down the union hall."

"Glory, I ain't plannin' on working in this shit hole until I retire. I'm gettin' in James Madison's dialysis tech program. I'm gonna get me a job soon's I graduate. They pay good money for dialysis techs."

"That's fine, Evie, you could keep on working here at James Madison, move up to the dialysis unit."

"Nah-ah, I'm fixing to work outside the city. My boyfriend works out at Lankenau. He says it's bee-utiful out there. All clean and modern. I'm gonna get my training and go work out at Swanky Lanky."

Gloria loaded two more bags into the machine, added the soap and set it in motion. "Well I'm goin' to the meeting. Even if you are planning on leaving this dump, you can still come. If we don't show any kinda unity, the new boss is gonna take away all our fricking benefits! Don't you know we got retirees worried they're gonna lose their pensions?"

Evie kept quiet, not wanting to disappoint her co-worker, but not wanting to make a promise she had no intention of keeping. She was on her way out of Philadelphia and on to a better life.

<><><>

Mimi poked her head into room 710 and asked the aide if she'd made up the A bed in 706, they were getting a new admission. "You know how they like to fill the beds," she said. "Half the time housekeeping is still wiping down the mattress when a new admit comes rolling into the room in a wheelchair asking for lunch."

"Yeah, I made the bed and I got an admission kit in the cabinet already," said Beatrice. "I hope we don't get another three-hundred pounder, this old back o' mine can't take no more of them double wide ones."

Mimi laughed at how Beatrice applied the term for an extra wide trailer to the morbidly obese patient. "No, this one's not going to be a big one. In fact he's lost weight, the doctors don't know why. It sounds like he could have cancer."

"That's a sorrowful shame." The aide came out of the room. "My aunt suffered terrible from cancer. She lasted near three years, though. Longer than the doctors gave her. God is merciful."

"Amen," said Mimi

As the nurse turned to go, Beatrice added that she'd straightened out the linen for the B-bed. "That lazy ass aide on three to eleven makes the sloppiest bed I ever seen. I make my admission beds tight."

"I know you do," said Mimi. "Your post-op beds are neat as a pin."

"Ya know in the old days our head nurse Miss Haab would drop a quarter on every admission bed. If'n it didn't bounce you had to make it up all over again. Oh, she was a tough head nurse. Tough, but fair."

"That was way before my time," said Mimi.

"Hospital's got to be the worst place in the world when you're sick," said the aide, going on to bathe another patient.

A medical student walked up to Mimi and asked if he could borrow an L-P set for a spinal tap.

"Is it for one of my patients?" the nurse asked,

"Uh, no, it's for a patient on Seven-North. The charge nurse there says their store room is out of L-P trays."

"What? You can't be taking trays from my store room for another floor, we have to charge every item or Central Stores won't replace it. You have to go down the basement and get it,"

"Basement?" said the student. "I didn't go to medical school to be some gopher for the nurses."

"Well I didn't go to nursing school to screw up my par level for some patient I can't charge for."

"Fine. I'll just tell my attending that you refused to help me provide needed care for my patient."

"Good. Be sure and get my name right, it's Mrs. Malone. R-N."

Watching the medical student go off in a huff, Mimi cursed her fate, stuck between the rigid hospital requirement to track and bill for every item they used on the ward and the needs of the staff to render care in a timely manner.

"Lord have mercy," she muttered and hurried to catch up on her morning rounds.

4

CEO Robert Reichart dropped the financial report on the conference table and cast a stern gaze at the managers seated around it. "We are following laws passed by the United States Congress regarding our fiduciary responsibilities for pension and defined benefit obligations. If those union idiots cannot manage their funds properly and allow their capital levels to fall below a safe level, they have no one to blame but themselves. I am under no obligation to bail out every mobbed up union when their leadership lines their pockets with members' money."

"You may be legally right, sir," said the Patient Relations director, "but morally I'm afraid you may be on thin ice. The public relations fallout will be horrendous if you go forward with your proposal."

"Nobody respects unions anymore," said Reichart. "The public understands we have to rein in health care costs, and labor is our biggest expense by far, it's a no-brainer." With a look of dismissal, he turned his attention to the performance report. He asked what the readmission rate had been for the previous month, knowing the federal government was monitoring the rate at which patients were readmitted to the hospital within thirty days of their discharge as a measure of effective treatment.

The numbers for James Madison were good, according to the Chief Financial Officer, but not good enough for the CEO.

"I want more resources put into follow-up phone calls to

the at-risk patients," he said. "The studies clearly demonstrate a drop in re-admission rates when primary services check up on their discharges." He turned to Miss Burgess, Director of Nursing. "How are we doing with our new visiting nurse program?"

Miss Burgess cleared her throat. She was still anxious whenever she had to report at the president's weekly operations meeting, having been spoiled by the easy going meetings she used to attend with the Chief Medical Officer, Dr. Roger Slocum, who shared her love of scotch.

"The new program has nearly doubled our number of weekly home visits. Our billable hours were one hundred and twenty for the last week of the month."

"How long are the insurers taking to pay us?" Martin said.

"Uh, I don't have those figures with me," said Burgess. "Perhaps..." She turned to the Chief Financial Officer.

"I can get that information to you as soon as I get back to my office," said the CFO. "Typically, Medicare takes ninety to one hundred twenty days to pay, assuming they accept the initial invoice without questioning it."

"We shouldn't be seeing any rejections from the third party payers," said Reichart. "My computerized diagnostic and billing program should hit the appropriate target categories every time."

"That is true in theory," said the CFO. "ADTP is a well-designed program, to be sure. But in practice we still see around a fifteen per cent rejection of the first reimbursement submission to Medicare."

Deciding he'd heard enough lame excuses for poor performance, Reichart dismissed the group and walked to his office, his footsteps silent in the administrative wing's plush carpet beneath his feet. The CEO had no patience for ineffective leaders. He had told his managers there were more cutbacks coming, including their own termination if they did not meet his benchmarks for "right-sizing" the workforce, including the highly paid Attending physicians. Reichart did not share with them the ten million dollar bonus he expected to receive when the benchmarks were met.

He found Joe West, Chief of Security, standing in the inner office. With a nod to West, Martin entered his inner sanctum, letting the security man close the door after following him in.

Declining an offered seat, West stood ramrod straight, a posture he'd learned in the military and continued while on the Philadelphia police force. His crisp, navy blue suit had creases as sharp as a knife, while his belt was ornamented by shiny handcuffs and a Glock pistol.

"What is the union response to my initiative?" asked Reichart.

"They are calling on their friends in the churches and the liberal press to support them," said West.

"Nothing more? No, they'll do something flashy, that hot head Lenny Moss will stir them up, you can be sure of that." Reichart eyed the security chief, whose dead shark eyes reflected the indifferent personality within. "I want eyes on him every minute he is on duty."

"Already in the works."

"I want ongoing video surveillance. I want audio recordings. Christ, if you can hack his phone, get me his text messages. I want that man out the door for good. Understand?"

"I have a better idea," said West. "Do you want to hear it?"

Reichart said nothing. He could be as cool and poker faced as West.

"How about a jail cell for the bastard?" said West. He told the CEO he was reasonably sure Moss would lead some kind of demonstration on hospital property. When he did, the security team would arrest him and bring charges. Asked what sort of charges, West listed resisting arrest, inciting a riot, assault on a hospital employee... maybe even criminal trespass.

"My friends on the force will run through the menu. By the time the DA has finished charging Moss and his buddies, he'll be facing a million dollar bail and felony charges."

"Good. Get it done." Reichart touched a key on his computer keyboard, bringing the screen to life. It was a sign he was done with West, who turned without a word and walked out. West wasn't bothered by the CEO's curt way of treating him. In fact, he admired it, having used the same approach on his men for years.

Exhausted, frightened and dying for a cup of coffee and a muffin, Anna Louisa sat outside Miss Burgess's office, having been told to return to the hospital right away, her hands restless on her lap. The Director of Nursing and the night supervisor were inside discussing the death in room 706. Anna knew she was going to face some kind of discipline, Mother Burgess showed no mercy when one of "her girls" screwed up. But it was so unfair! Anna couldn't understand how her patient could have gone into rigor so quickly after death. She wondered if he had some kind of medical condition that caused his connective tissue and muscles to lock up so rapidly.

The secretary's phone rang. She picked it up, listened, said, "Yes, Miss Burgess," and nodded to the nurse.

Getting up from her chair, Anna Louisa felt dizzy for a moment. She grasped the edge of the desk until her head cleared, then she squared her shoulders as her grandmother always told her to do, held her chin up and vowed to herself not to cry in front of Burgess. Better to sit in silence then let her voice tremble and lose control.

In the room Miss Burgess sat splayed in her big leather chair. Anna couldn't help but think that, were the Director a patient on her ward, she would need an extra-wide wheelchair to transport her.

The night supervisor, Miss D'Lorenzo, was standing behind the desk beside Burgess. The dreaded incident report was open on the desk in front of them. Beside it was Mr. Landry"s chart. As Anna glanced at the items she saw a strange computer printout she didn't recognize.

Feeling the dizziness return, Anna decided to take the chair in front of the desk, even though no one had invited her to sit.

"I have reviewed the reports and looked over the patient's medical records," said Burgess. "By all accounts the patient who died was in stable condition. He was scheduled for discharge to home today, he'd completed his chemotherapy, isn't that right?"

With a lump in her throat, Anna Louisa nodded yes, not yet trusting her voice.

"We do not yet have the postmortem results, of course, that will take some time. But the lab results drawn by the code team are deeply disturbing." Burgess leaned forward, her black eyes menacing and cold. "Do you have any idea what the dead man's blood glucose level was?"

Anna shook her head.

Burgess held up her hand with thumb and first finger joined in a circle.

"Zero."

The young nurse's mouth dropped open. "But, but how can that be, Mister Landry was not diabetic."

"That's precisely the point!" said D'Lorenzo. "Your patient did not have any diabetic medications in his drug profile."

"But he did have them in his medication tray," Burgess said. She withdrew a plastic bag from the pharmacy with a bottle of regular insulin in it. "When pharmacy made the morning exchange, this was found in Landry's medication tray. On your cart!"

Anna's head ached and her dizziness returned. She could not understand how insulin could be placed in Mr. Landry's bin, the pharmacy filled all the prescription orders, there was no reason to supply a drug the patient would not receive.

"It is clear to us that your patient died due to your administration of insulin to a non-diabetic," said Burgess. "No doubt the autopsy will explain the eventual cause of death. Possibly a heart attack or stroke. But whatever the final cause, it is clear that your grievous medication error led to this unfortunate man's death."

Anna's throat was too constricted for her to speak. Her eyes welled up in tears.

"Have you anything to say in your defense?"

Anna looked from Burgess to the night supervisor and back to Burgess. Her mouth was dry as burned toast. She felt a terrible panic, as if she were falling down, down through a hole in the floor into some cold, black pit.

"I...I don't know how it could have happened," said Anna, her voice weak and tremulous. "I did not administer insulin to any patient on my shift. I don't understand why insulin would be in his drawer."

"Not only did you give the wrong patient insulin," said D'Lorenzo, "but you failed to check on him on your hourly rounds. If you had, you might have realized he was going into hypoglycemic shock."

"Miss Burgess, I made my rounds every hour, like I always do. On my last rounds, the six am one, he was sleeping peacefully, I'm sure of it."

"Don't lie to us!" said Miss D'Lorenzo. "It's bad enough when a nurse fails in her duties and doesn't follow a simple protocol, but lying about what you did and falsifying your nursing notes make the crime all that much worse."

"I'm not lying Miss D'Lorenzo! I swear by the Blessed Virgin, the patient was sleeping and breathing normally at six in the morning!"

The supervisor scowled and glanced at Burgess, who pulled a form from a folder. She arranged the form so that it was perfectly square on her blotter, took a pen from a holder and scribbled her name on the bottom of the form.

"You are hereby officially terminated as of today. You will receive a certified letter in the mail detailing the offenses you have committed, and payroll will send you your final paycheck."

"I'm sorry, Miss Burgess, I'm so sorry," said Anna. "If you fire me I will have a very hard time finding another job, all the hospitals are laying nurses off."

"What makes you think you will ever work in this profession again?" said Burgess. "You can kiss your license to practice nursing good-bye. When the board hears about your negligent behavior I have no doubt in my mind they will revoke your license to practice in the Commonwealth of Pennsylvania."

As the terrified nurse sat trembling, D'Lorenzo walked up to her, roughly pulled the ID badge from Anna's uniform and dropped it like a malodorous specimen onto Burgess's desk.

Without a further word, Anna rose slowly from her

chair, turned and shuffled out of the office. A security guard waiting for her in the hall handed the nurse a plastic trash bag with the contents of her locker. "This way," he told her. The guard led Anna to the hospital main entrance and stood watching as the nurse passed through the automatic doors and slowly made her was down the broad marble steps. Anna stood at the bus stop on Germantown Ave for several moments, fighting back tears, not knowing what to do next.

5

Moose Maddox pushed the food cart down the Seven South hall collecting the lunch trays. He finished his rounds at the little pantry, where several dirty trays were stacked on the counter. After clearing off the stainless steel counter he ran a damp rag over it.

"You trying to take my job?" came a voice from the hallway, "'cause I'll have to file a grievance with the union if you keep that crap up."

Moose turned and saw Lenny standing there watching him.

"Heh, heh. Just tryin' not to leave too many crumbs for the mice," said Moose.

"Hey, everybody's got to eat, even the rodents." said Lenny.

As Moose closed the door of the food cart and began pushing it down toward the service elevator, he asked Lenny what he thought would happen at the union meeting that afternoon.

"Bad news, very bad news and horrendously bad news," said Lenny.

"Come on, is it really that bad?"

Following Moose to the service elevator, Lenny took a moment to think how to frame his answer. "It's that bad, Moose, because the bosses are not gonna quit until they take every last fricking benefit away from us."

"But we got a contract."

"We had a contract. When Croesus bought the hospital

and converted it to a for-profit facility, the new management they put in claimed the old contract doesn't apply to them."

"That ain't right. It can't be."

"Right or wrong, it's the game they're playing and they're playing for keeps. But that's not the worst of it."

"I know, I heard. They wanna take away our pensions and health benefits."

"James Madison, Temple, Hahnemann, they're all crying poverty. They want to get out of paying into the pension and benefit fund. If they do that, the fund will be bankrupt inside of a year."

"Damn. They can do that? That's legal?"

Lenny punched the elevator button for his friend. "It's the law, Moose. If the money in our pension fund drops below a certain threshold they're allowed to bail on us. They say the fund is almost at the magic number."

Moose pushed the cart into the elevator, pressed the button for the basement and sent the cart on its way to the kitchen. Heading to Seven North for their cart, he put his big hand on Lenny's shoulder. "We got people working down the kitchen, got all kind of medical problems. Old Laurence had a heart attack last year, Molly B had cancer... They have to have their health insurance."

"I know, Moose, I've been hearing the same complaints everywhere I go."

"We're gonna fight it, ain't we? The union's gonna kick some ass, right?"

"Of course they'll fight it. But the law in this case is on the boss's side."

"We'll it ain't right, man. We lose our health benefits and our pension, it's 'bout gonna kill us."

<><><>

Mimi had just settled her new patient, Mr. Manwatty, a soft spoken young man from India, into room 706 and shown him how to operate the bed controls, including how to turn on the TV, when she heard a knock on the door.

"Can we come in?" asked a soft-spoken physician, a troupe of residents and medical students in tow.

"Just finished, Doctor Bilici," said Mimi. She patted the patient on the shoulder and squeezed her way through the medical team in the doorway.

Dr. Galen Bilici led his team on the Hospitalist Service into the room. He was a slightly built man, prematurely bald, with a handsome face and warm eyes. After rubbing a dollop of alcohol gel on his hands, the Attending physician stepped to the bedside and shook the patient's hand.

"I am Doctor Bilici, this is my team. I understand you have not been feeling yourself of late."

"Thank you, doctor," said Manwatty. "No, I have been feeling very fatigued. I have no appetite at all, I only take a little soup and crackers."

As the patient reported his story, Bilici looked over the slender young man, noting how the patient let his arms lie at his side as if they were a burden to lift. Bilici indicated to one of the medical students to examine the patient. She lifted Manwatty's hospital gown and gently pressed his abdomen, eliciting a sharp breath. She listened to his heart and lungs, then stepped aside while her Attending took his turn listening to the quiet sounds of air flowing in and out of the lungs.

"We have some of your lab results back," said Bilici. "I'm going to order more today, so the nurse will have to stick you one more time. I'm sorry."

"That is all right, doctor, I know it is all part of the process. I will never complain when someone is trying to help me."

Leading his team out to the corridor, Bilici turned to the intern, a slender young woman who had been a competitive swimmer in college, as she recounted the new patient's history.

"Mister Sanjay Manwatty is a twenty-three year old college student. He was born and raised in India, where he was immunized for the common childhood diseases. He has no significant medical history, he has never been hospitalized, and he was in his normal state of health until he developed fatigue, malaise, nausea and generalized muscle pain."

"Chest x-ray?" asked Bilici.

"His chest film doesn't show any interstitial infiltrates or cavitary lesions. His white count is eleven-thousand and his urine showed a high degree of sedimentation.

"Fever?" Bilici asked.

"His T-max in the ER was one hundred one point four."

When their Attending asked for possible diagnoses, the intern noted that the ER physician had made a diagnosis of cholangitis.

"The ER doctor is always wrong," said Bilici. "What is in our differential?"

"Malaria," said another one of the interns.

"Viral syndrome," said the resident. "We should run a PCR for viral proteins."

"What about liver flukes, he has diffuse abdominal pain," said one of the students."

Bilici noted the patient had been living in the US for three years and thought a parasite should be low on their differential. "Has he been vaccinated for TB?"

The intern said she believed he'd been vaccinated for

TB, but the vaccination history was unclear. Bilici said, "If Mister Manwatty was vaccinated for TB, there's no point in running a PPD test, it would return a false positive, the test lacks specificity in these patients."

"What about isolation?" asked one of the medical students. "Should we order respiratory precautions?"

"That's a good thought. Right now TB is way down on my differential. Besides, the chest x-ray was essentially clear, wasn't it? That rules out pulmonary TB ." The intern confirmed the initial report had been 'mostly clear,' the final report was pending.

After discussing several more possible diagnoses, Dr. Bilici told the Fellow to read what ADTP, the Advanced Diagnostic and Treatment Program, suggested. The program, dubbed "teepee" by the staff, had selected a long list of possible diagnoses, ranking them in order from most likely to least. Attached to each possible diagnosis was a list of further tests to be ordered.

Bilici looked over the Fellow's shoulder, frowning. "Hmm, that's a very long list."

"Do we have to order all those tests?" the female intern asked.

"Yes and no," said Bilici. "Technically the computer makes 'recommendations.' But if you don't order one of them and in the end that failure leads to a delay in diagnosis, or worse, to medical complications, you will be roasted alive by the performance improvement people. And of course, the family will sue you from now until you give up your practice and get a job at a McDonalds flipping burgers."

"No wonder medical care is so expensive in this country," the intern said.

"Ours is not to reason why, ours is to cover our ass," said Bilici. The Attending instructed his team to order several, but not all, of the recommended tests. Then he told the intern to put in a consult for the Infectious Disease service. "Who's on service this month?"

The intern stared at the computer screen, scrolling through the menu. "Ah, here it is, Doctor Auginello. Is he any good?"

Bilici smiled the smile of a well-fed gastronome. "Any good? He's only the chief of the Infectious Disease division and possibly the best internal medicine doctor in the house. Yes, I would say Doctor Auginello is any good."

6

Mimi smiled when she saw Dr. Michael Auginello and his Infectious Disease team approach the Seven South nursing station.

"Hi, Doctor Auginello. Here to see the new admit in seven-o-six?"

"That's the one," he said, reading the name on one of the 3x5 cards he carried in his lab coat pocket. "How is he doing?"

"Ok, I guess. He has a low grade fever and some abdominal discomfort, but it isn't severe."

"They didn't send a urine culture in the ER, would you collect one for me?" he said.

"Sure thing. You want a clean voided specimen or should I straight-cath him?"

"Let's go with a voided specimen for now and see what it shows."

Auginello told his team that when he was a medical student all of the wards had mini-labs, with microscopes and basic testing instruments. "You could spin down a blood sample and look at it under the microscope right there on rounds. I learned more from those on-site labs than in my micro lectures. Progress."

He led his team to Manwatty's room and stood outside the doorway. "Tell me about the patient," he said to his resident.

The resident reviewed the information supplied by the ER and the Hospitalist Service, then continued with the results of his own physical exam and scrutiny of the lab work. When he was finished, the ID Attending asked for possible diagnoses. The team came up with half a dozen, from infected gall bladder to viral gastroenteritis.

"What about bovine TB?" asked the ID Fellow, noting that the clear chest x-ray precluded a diagnosis of pulmonary tuberculosis.

"It's unlikely he ingested unpasteurized milk from a cow with active tuberculosis while living in Philadelphia," said Auginello, smiling at the Fellow's out-of-the-box suggestion. "But l agree, we need to keep TB in the differential until the case comes into focus." He went on to ask for treatment recommendations.

"Broad spectrum antibiotics," said the resident. "Symptomatic relief of fever and headache...CAT scan if the symptoms worsen and do not respond to treatment."

When the medical student asked about anti-fungal treatment, Auginello suggested waiting to see if the patient responded to the antibiotics first, reminding them that the anti-fungals carried some serious potential side effects, renal failure being just one of them. Then he led them into the patient's room.

"Mister Manwatty, my name is Doctor Auginello. I'm with the Infectious Disease service. Doctor Bilici asked me to see you."

The young man sat up in bed and reached out a hand. Auginello noted that the young man's palm was dry and the grip, weak. "Thank you for seeing me, doctor. I am sorry to cause you so much trouble. All of these doctors on my case..."

"Don't think about that, this is a teaching hospital. It's we who are grateful to you for giving us the opportunity to treat you and to learn from your case."

Auginello took out his stethoscope, wiped the diaphragm with an alcohol pad and pressed it gently on the patient's chest, listening first to the heart tones, then, the lungs. When he listened to the bowel sounds, he asked if there was any abdominal pain.

"Yes, a little."

The doctor's pressing on the abdomen elicited a wince of pain.

"Have you lost any weight in the last month?"

"Yes, I have lost ten pounds. I have no appetite."

Auginello pressed on the patient's ankle, looking for signs of edema. "I understand you believe you were vaccinated for TB in your home country," said Auginello. "Is that right?"

"I think so, doctor. I have written to my mother. Perhaps she can answer the question with confidence."

"Well if you receive the information, tell your nurse and she can make a note in the chart and I'll hear about it. All right? Anything we can get for you?"

"No, thank you, doctor, I am grateful for all that you have done for me."

Auginello led his team out to the hall, where they gathered once more for a summary of the findings. As the Attending made comments about how to test for the different possible diagnoses, Doctor Roger Slocum, the Chief Medical Officer, came by with his administrative assistant.

"Michael. How are ID rounds this month?"

Auginello knew that the Chief was as much interested in the revenue stream that the ID service was generating as the efficacy of the treatments they recommended.

"It's been a busy month, Roger, we're getting consults from every department."

"Well good. It's good to be busy. If you want a job done well ask a busy person, eh?"

In response to Dr. Slocum's question about the case

they were currently discussing, Auginello told him the signs and symptoms to date were insufficiently specific to render a diagnosis.

"Hasn't the ADTP program given you the answer yet?"

Auginello's face took on a pained expression. He told Slocum that the computer program had coughed up twenty different possible diagnoses, but even its mega-brain was not smart enough to identify one disease with a ninety percent confidence.

"I believe we will arrive at the correct diagnosis first," said the ID Fellow, a mild mannered gentleman from Equador who had trained in Cuba, later transferring to a US program.

"Is that a challenge?" Slocum said.

Auginello put out a hand to shake. "Yes, by god, it is. I'll spring for dinner for the administrative staff if Teepee comes up with the correct diagnosis first."

"And dinner for the ID service if you do it first? Fine, it's a bet. But I don't want to hear you've taken the money out of your departmental budget. This comes out of your pocket."

The Chief strutted off, confident that the computer system would vanquish Auginello, a mere mortal. The infectious disease physician had only the memory of a mortal man; the computer had a universe of knowledge.

Mimi watched the encounter with a rising sense of excitement. She knew many of the Attendings were angry that Teepee was robbing them of their autonomy and their authority. Good for Dr. Auginello to stand up to the CMO, the man was a gofer for the big bosses. The nurse just hoped Dr. Auginello won the contest, it would be a terrible thing if the damn computer beat him.

<><><>

When Anna picked up her daughter from the school bus stop, Maribel was delighted to see her mother at the bus stop. Usually Anna Louisa was sleeping in the afternoon after working the long night shift and their neighbor Katrina met the bus for her and Katrina's son Gabriel.

"Mommy!" she cried, running to Anna and throwing her arms around her mother.

Wearing sunglasses to conceal her red, teary eyes, Anna said nothing. When Maribel took her mother's hand, Anna barely grasped the little girl's fingers.

Looking up at her mother, Maribel said, "Mommy, aren't you happy to see me? You didn't give me a kiss!"

"I'm sorry, cariño, of course I'm glad to see my baby girl. I just had a bad day at work is all." She bent down and kissed the top of Maribel's head.

"Did somebody die?" asked Melody. "Is that why you are sad?"

"Si, somebody died. Somebody is always dying in the hospital."

They walked together for several minutes in silence. When Maribel asked her mother if they could stop for an ice cream cone or a slice of mango pie, Anna told her they were not stopping today for anything. The girl had never seen her mother so serious and quiet.

In the middle of a block, Anna suddenly stopped walking. She realized she had been so concerned about her own punishment, she hadn't taken the time to say a prayer for the poor patient Mr. Landry who died, something she always did when a patient on the ward passed or was facing a very difficult procedure. Anna felt the staff should always mourn for their patient who died, even if they did not often have a chance to attend the funeral, as nurses had done back in the old days.

I have been selfish, she told herself. I think only of myself. She made a vow to go to church in the morning, where she would light a candle for Mr. Landry, and then she would take confession. Anna made a silent promise to be kinder to her patients and not to think only about herself and her troubles.

If she ever was able to work in the nursing profession again.

Oh my god, she thought, what will happen when Jimmy finds out? For sure he will ask for custody of Maribel. That would be terrible.

The rest of the walk home was without conversation.

When Lenny and Moose walked into the union building on Germantown Ave, they were surprised to see a throng of retirees waiting to go upstairs to the meeting. The one elevator could only hold three or four people at a time, and several of the retired workers used walkers or canes. A few of them had oxygen tanks on little wheels dragging behind them.

A thickly built dark haired woman in a wheelchair caught Lenny's eye. "Big Mary!" he called out, rushing over to the laundry worker who had suffered a stroke on the job and gone out on medical disability. Her right arm and leg were paralyzed, the hand frozen in a permanent fist. Betty, a retired housekeeper who used to work on Lenny's ward, was behind the wheelchair waiting to help her friend into the elevator.

"You look great, Mary, really great," said Lenny.

Mary reached out her good hand and took Lenny's hand. She held it for a long moment, working to summon up her words.

"Good...good, Lenny."

Betty patted Big Mary on the shoulder. "It's okay, baby, we know you missed Lenny more'n all the rest of us. He asks about you all the time."

"I'm so sorry I haven't been out to see you in, what has it been, three, four months?" said Lenny.

Big Mary released Lenny's hand and held up her hand with five fingers extended.

"Five? Really, has it been that long? Aw, I'm sorry, Mary, I'll get out to the nursing home soon as I can."

"She ain't in the home no more," said Betty. "Big Mary's back home living with her daughter and her gran'. They taking good care of her."

"That's fabulous! I'm so happy for you." Lenny gave his friend a hug, then he thanked her for coming to the meeting. "I've got to go upstairs, I'll see you in the hall." He hurried up the stairs and joined Moose, who was talking to several dietary workers.

"Yo, Lenny," said Stella, a former dietary worker, now retired for ten years. "You gonna stand up and say something about the contract? 'Cause if'n you don't I'm gonna whoop you something terrible with this cane o' mine." She held up a knobby wooden cane, stained black and lethal looking.

"Harry is gonna take charge of this meeting, it's his show, let's see what he says."

"He gonna fight it, ain't he?" asked Stella.

"We are going to fight it," said Lenny. "I do miss you working in the cafeteria. It seems like the service has gone to crap since you left. "

"Don't try none o' your sweet talk on me, Lenny Moss. Save it for that lovely wife of yours. How's she doing? "

"Fine, thanks, I'll tell Patience you were asking about her." He walked to the side of the room and looked at his people. He saw a rainbow of colors, each department identified by the color of their scrub suits or work clothes. The ward clerks sported dress casual attire. Many of the retirees were dressed in their best Sunday going to church clothes, not wanting their former coworkers to think they had fallen on hard times, though many of them were barely getting by.

When Betty pushed Big Mary in her wheelchair down

the center aisle to a place in the front, everyone seated on the aisle reached out and patted Mary's arm or squeezed her hand. They remembered the terrible heat wave that had clamped its hand over Philadelphia, making the laundry an unbearable hell to work in. Lenny had asked the supervisor to let the laundry workers switch to the night shift, when it was cooler. The supervisor liked the idea but had been overruled by the senior administrator, who was unwilling to pay the shift differential that the night tour required.

Big Mary suffered a stroke while working in the laundry during that brutal heat wave, leading to a walkout by the laundry workers and an eventual resolution to the issue, though it came too late to save Mary from her injury.

As Lenny took a seat beside Moose, Steve Fender, the VP for organizing, stepped to the stage and tested the microphone. "All right, brothers and sisters, let's all take a seat, we've got a lot to talk about today, put your butts in a chair and quiet down."

The chatter died down to a low murmur as the last of the retirees slowly made their way to their seats.

"First off," said the VP, "I know everyone is concerned about the rumors that the hospital is going to withdraw its participation in the benefits and pension fund. Without going into too many details, let me just say—"

"You aren't gonna let them take away our benefits, are you?" called out a retiree from the back.

An uproar filled the room as current workers and retirees all called out, demanding to know what was going to happen. The union VP held his hands out for quiet, but the crowd would not be silenced.

Gloria Green leapt to her feet, shouting, "This is a load o' crap! They take away my prescription benefits, I got to choose between feeding my body and treating my illness!"

"You tell 'em, Glory!" a coworker yelled his agreement.
"I starve or I die from sugar diabetes, high blood pressure and a whole lot more ailments!" Gloria shook her fist, her eyes wide with fury. As she sat down, she was surprised and pleased to see her coworker Evie sitting a few rows behind her.

Another member stood up, an oxygen tube around his face. "I can't yell like the rest o' you, but I sure can make a ruckus!" He beat on his oxygen tank with his cane, raising a loud clamor. The other members cheered and applauded him.

Unable to bring the members and retirees to order, the VP stepped to the edge of the stage, leaned over and spoke to his assistant, a slender woman in high heels, who hurried out of the hall.

Another member yelled out, asking what the union was doing to protect their union benefits. The VP began to explain that the other big hospitals — Temple, Hahnemann, Jefferson — were all threatening the same withdrawal of financial support.

"We know what they're doin'!" cried a retiree, waiving her cane high in the air. "We want to know what you're gonna do to stop it!"

After another bout of shouting and finger pointing, a slim, silver haired gentleman entered the hall and walked slowly up the center aisle. He walked tall and ramrod straight, despite his seventy years of age and his countless battles against bosses, cops, police dogs and racists, from Mobile to Memphis and many points north. As he walked down the center aisle the crowd grew quiet.

Harry Echols, president of the hospital service workers union, skipped up the steps to the stage two at a time and reached for the microphone at the podium. He looked out over the crowd, his dark, handsome face lit in a broad smile of delight and satisfaction. Chuckling, he said, "I got a little story for y'all, if you'll give me a few minutes of your time."

He waited, enjoying the silence that slowly descended over the crowd.

"Last week I was at a union meeting in a hotel out in Harrisburg. Oh, there were big wigs from all the other unions. Young ones and middle aged ones...a whole passel of union folks. Well, after lunch we had to go up six flights to a breakout session, and one of the elevators was out of order. There was only one working elevator, and the line to get in it stretched all the way down the hallway."

Echols chuckled again, took out a lavender handkerchief from the pocket of his double breasted suit and wiped his forehead. "So I said to the young whipper-snappers, "C'mon, boys, let's take the stairs, and I proceeded to open the door to the stairwell and climb up those steps."

"Go ahead, Harry!" called one of the women.

"I jog five miles a day every day, rain or shine," Echols said. "And those young union people, by the time they got to the sixth floor, they were panting and sweating and kinda wobbly on their legs, but I was breathin' easy and smiling. So don't you retirees in this meeting stop gettin' out and walking and doing your exercises. Take that oxygen tank with you, but get out and walk!"

He wiped his face again and adopted a serious look on his face. "Brothers and sisters, I've been fighting for worker rights my whole life. I've seen a lot of dirty, low down scurrilous behavior on the part of the bosses. I've seen the fire trucks come out and threaten to turn the hoses on us for setting up a picket line at Jimmy Giuffre's hospital!"

"That's right!" cried a retiree who had been on that picket line.

"Old Frank Rizzo was ready to order the hoses turned

on our people, but Jimmy Giuffre told him not to do it, he didn't want his people hurt, so they put away the hoses and drove the fire trucks back to the station and let the union in.

"I've seen hard times, brothers and sisters, but I've never seen times as hard and desperate as what I'm seeing today here in Philadelphia."

Heads nodded, voices murmured their agreement.

"And what all this means for us, for the workers on the job and for the retired workers who depend on their little bitty pension check and their health benefits and their prescription benefits, is we have got to fight harder and longer, and with more serious commitment to the cause of the rights of labor than we have ever done before. We have to fight at the workplace, we have to fight at City Hall, we have to fight in Harrisburg, and we have to win, because the price we will pay for losing is our death, and I am not, brothers and sisters, going to let my people die from poverty and a lack of medical care when there is plenty of money to pay for the benefits and the defined pensions that you have worked and sweated for and earned with your years of service!"

The crowd stood up, cheering and applauding. They stamped their canes and their feet, held each other's hands and laughed and cried.

Echols went on to say that the union had already reached out to the social justice organizations that they had supported for so many decades, the faith based groups, the immigrant rights groups, the literacy schools and the arts programs. They were calling on the community to support the union in its hour of desperate need.

"Each and every single one of you has got to go out to your church, to your children and your grandchildren's schools; go out to your block associations and your local newspapers and local TV and radio stations. Tell them what the bosses are threatening to do to you, and ask them for their support."

"We're with you Harry!" cried an old member. "Just like in seventy-three!"

"And when we schedule a rally to call attention to our cause, I want all of you and all your co-workers and family to meet me here at the union hall. We're going to have the biggest, loudest, rocking-est demonstration this city has seen in twenty years. We'll march down to City Hall and let the politicians know what those greedy bastards in their ivory towers are trying to do to us!"

After the cheers and the whooping and the hollering died down, Harry turned the meeting over to the VP for signing up members for various committees and assignments. Echols skipped down the steps and walked along the side of the crowd. He stopped where Lenny and Moose were sitting and gestured for the two of them to follow him out into the anteroom. Lenny looked at Moose, who shrugged and rose to his feet.

Out in the hall, Echols faced the two hospital workers. "Lenny. Moose. You guys know, the union has to give a thirty day notice to the hospital before it takes any direct action at the work site. Our hands are tied, it's a violation of the contract if we march on James Madison or Temple without giving due notice."

Lenny knew about the provision in the contract that required the union to give the administration a heads up long before they brought any mass demonstration to the hospital. Moose pointed out that if the new management was refusing to honor the contract, the union shouldn't have to either.

"I wish I could go along with that," said Echols, "but we're arguing in court that the old contract is still in effect.

How's it going to look if we say honor the contract with one hand and we ignore it with the other?"

When Moose admitted the logic of the president's position, Echols explained that he couldn't call for a march on the facility without the thirty day warning. But Lenny and Moose could.

"You talkin' wildcat strike," said Moose. "That's serious shit."

"Not a strike," said Echols. "Not yet. But a big demonstration with all the current workers, the retirees, their families and friends, ministers and rabbis — anyone and everyone we can bring down to the hospital."

"Are you calling for actions at all the hospitals we represent, or just James Madison?" asked Lenny,

"James Madison will be the first, and the biggest, we have the most militant workers there."

"And you know why they're so strong," said Moose.

Echols smiled a Cheshire cat grin. "Everybody knows, Moose. I'll never forget what Lenny has done for the union." He leaned in on Lenny and asked would he lead the demonstration.

Lenny thought a moment, having learned from decades of union struggles that every proposal had to be worked over, even the ones that sounded like no-brainers.

"Harry, I need to know what exactly you're asking us to do. I mean, a lot of the retirees are physically disabled. I can't ask them to do something that could get them thrown in jail, or worse, get their heads cracked or their face pepper-sprayed."

"No, no, it's nothing like that. You just lead them to the hospital and hold a rally outside. No arrests. No occupying the president's office this time."

"Sometimes occupying the office is the only way to get their attention," said Lenny.

"But not with the retirees," said Echols. Lenny agreed, he would organize no sit-in with retirees.

"Then it's settled," said Echols. "You rally outside the hospital on public property, we get some news coverage, and everybody goes home safe and intact."

Lenny arched a single black eyebrow, puzzled. "When's it gonna be?"

"Saturday, our people go to church on Sunday."

As Lenny and Moose turned to leave, President Echols added, "And no more Nazi references in your flyers!"

8

As she began her day shift, Mimi was thankful for small favors. The night nurse who replaced Anna Louisa hadn't left any serious problems to deal with, none of the diabetics had low blood sugars this morning, and the only STAT order was for a medication she had in the stock cabinet, which meant she wouldn't have to send her aide down to the pharmacy right in the middle of breakfast.

The day was humming along until she heard the dispatcher's voice on the GPS unit she wore around her neck tell her, "Room seven-o-five needs assistance." Great. Assistance. What kind of assistance, she muttered to herself. God forbid the dispatcher would supply any more information than a damn room number.

Closing and locking her rolling medication cart, she walked to room 705, knowing a computer was tracking and timing her movements through the GPS unit the nurses were forced to wear. Should she take more than four minutes to reach the room, the computer would ding her and she'd get an email stating that her performance was below the nursing director's standard.

"Good thing I don't have to pee," she said loud enough for the dispatcher to hear.

In the room she found the A bed soiled by loose stool and a trail of brown spots leading to the bathroom. Opening the door, she saw a tearful Miss Gittens sitting on the toilet, her head in her hands.

"I'm sorry, Mimi, I'm so sorry!" Miss Gittens said when

she saw the nurse.

Mimi told her it was okay, it wasn't her fault, it was the darn bowel prep they gave her. "That stuff is too strong for elderly patients like you. I keep telling the GI doctor, but he likes how clean it makes your colon, he can see everything he needs to see."

Miss Gittens took Mimi's hand and patted it. "You're a good Christian soul, Mimi my dear, a good Christian soul."

Assured that the patient needed no help cleaning herself, Mimi stepped carefully around the trail of stool to bundle up the soiled linen and carry it to a laundry bag out in the hall, holding the smelly sheets away from her body. In the hall she spied Lenny running a dry mop along the corridor.

"Yo, Lenny! I got an incontinent patient in seven-o-five, would you run a mop over the floor?"

Lenny gave her a wave in acknowledgement and made his way to the housekeeping closet, where his trusty mop and bucket awaited. He poured in some detergent, added bleach and filled it with hot water, then pushed it out into the hall. Another morning in paradise, he mused, wondering what other delights awaited him.

As he ran the mop across the stool-splattered floor, Miss Gittens sat up in a chair and watched him.

"Do you enjoy your work, young man?" she asked.

"I do," said Lenny. "Every day is a surprise, you never know what's going to need your attention. It's never the same."

"A good job is a blessing, my mother always used to say. Hard to find, harder to keep."

Advising the woman to wait until the floor was fully dry before walking on it, he rolled his bucket out to the hall.

"Thanks, Lenny!" Mimi called to him from her med cart.

As Lenny set up the yellow CAUTION - WET FLOOR

sign in the doorway, Mimi asked him if he had a minute. He pushed his mop and bucket against the wall out of the traffic bustling through the busy corridor and waited.

"It's about my friend Anna Louisa, the girl they fired yesterday. Lenny, it's way worse than I thought, they're saying she didn't just fail to check on her patient and see that he had expired, they say she gave the patient an insulin overdose!"

"Don't the nurses check the sugar on their diabetic patients?"

"That's just it, Mister Landry wasn't diabetic. Pharmacy found an open bottle of insulin in his med tray, they change them every morning at seven a.m. Now they're saying she didn't just give the wrong medication, but she didn't check on him on her hourly rounds and then falsified her nursing notes to say she had."

"So they terminated her," said Lenny.

Mimi nodded her head. "Since Croesus came in and took over the hospital, nursing has been firing staff right and left." Mimi glanced down at the GPS unit hanging on a thick band, knowing that the dispatcher might be listening, the nurses never knew what they heard. "Right and left."

"We're getting hammered hard, too," said Lenny. "James Madison is threatening to stop paying into our union benefit and pension plan. The retirees will lose everything."

"I heard about that! Hahnemann and Temple are talking about doing the same thing. It's awful."

Mimi stepped closer to Lenny, dropping her voice to a whisper. Not that it would keep the dispatchers from hearing if they chose to eavesdrop.

"I am ab-so-lutely sure my girl did not miss checking the patient in seven-o-six, and she did not give him any insulin." Seeing a skeptical look on Lenny's face, she said,

"To tell you the god's honest truth, there are some nurses on staff I'd walk away from and believe they falsified their nursing notes. But Anna isn't the type to falsify her nursing notes. I mean, she stays over an hour every shift to check off every little thing on the computer. It just couldn't happen."

"Didn't you tell me yesterday you found the patient in rigor mortis on your first rounds that morning?"

"Yeah, I did," said Mimi, sounding disheartened. "But there's got to be an explanation that gets Anna her job back!"

Lenny looked down at the old marble floor, noting the cracks that came with age, like the lines on the faces of the elderly patients. As a union steward he'd heard complaints like Mimi's for years. Decades. It was always the same, a worker swore they weren't out of their work area without authorization, even though a half dozen co-workers saw him there. Or they really did punch in their time card at the start of a shift, even though the video camera above the time clock showed someone else punching in for him. They swore on a stack of bibles they were innocent, and sometimes they were. More to the point, they almost never deserved the level of punishment meted out to them. But justice wasn't written into the hospital by-laws.

"Lenny, you've helped so many people in this god forsaken place, can't you help Anna? She has a young daughter! If she loses her nursing license, I don't know how she'll get by."

Lenny wanted to help, his instinct was to step up whenever a worker was in trouble, whatever the cause. But the nurse wasn't in his union. She wasn't in any union. And the case against her sounded air tight.

"I don't represent her, she's not in my bargaining unit," he said.

50

"That didn't keep you from representing Pauline, remember? She was in trouble big time and you went with her to meet with Miss Burgess and the administration, and you got her termination rescinded!"

"Yeah, I did, but that was a special circumstance, Pauline was being stalked by a psycho, she ended up almost dying. This case...it really sounds like the nurse has got nothing to defend herself with." When he saw Mimi was about to come back with another argument, he added that he had his hands full organizing the current and the retired workers around their fight to keep the hospital from wiping out their pensions and health benefits.

"But this idea she left a dead patient in bed for hours and didn't check him on her hourly rounds, it can't be true, Lenny! Like I said, there's gotta be some explanation for the rigor and the low blood sugar. Maybe the patient had some weird medical condition that locked up his joints prematurely. Some-thing." Mimi looked into Lenny's dark eyes, searching for sympathy. For a change of heart.

Lenny took in a long breath. He liked Mimi. More than that, he knew she was a smart woman who didn't put up with anybody's bull shit. Although he believed she was wrong about her friend's innocence, Mimi's flat out assertion that the nurse had been wrongly terminated had him wondering: could there be more to the story than what he'd been told? Besides, he couldn't stand idly by while a hospital worker was unfairly fired.

"All right, here's what I'll do. I'll try to get some information about how the man died, and when he died. And I'll see what I can find out about this early rigor mortis situation. Not that I know anything about medicine, but we'll see."

"Oh, great, thank you, Lenny! And you'll call Anna Louisa and get her side of the story, won't you?"

Agreeing to call the nurse, Lenny was surprised to see Mimi hold out a piece of paper with Anna's phone number and address on it. "I told her this could be a criminal matter, so you would be calling on her."

When he raised a single, quizzical eyebrow at her outstretched hand, Mimi laughed. "You shouldn't be surprised, I have confidence in you, Lenny, I know all about your loving heart."

Moose Maddox pushed the food cart down Seven South handing out breakfast trays. Beatrice joined him, carrying one tray for every two that he handled.

"Hey, Moose," the aide said. "Am I really gonna lose my health benefits? My boy has seizures, he has to have his prescription and his doctor visits."

Moose told her about the planned "spontaneous" demonstration scheduled for Saturday and asked her to quietly spread the word. "Be careful who you tell, they got snitches in every department," said Moose.

"No worries, I know who's for real and who's crappin' on me. I'll be there. With my boy!"

He brought a tray to Mrs. Gershawn in 705, but had none for her roommate, who sniffed the air when he uncovered her roommate's tray, a wistful look on her face.

"I'm going for a test today," she told him. "Will I get breakfast when I'm back?"

"Of course," said Moose. "Ask Mimi to call down the kitchen, I'll bring something up to you."

Miss Gittens smiled and lay back in bed, waiting for her time to go for the test.

Seeing Lenny emptying trash liners into a rolling cart, Moose told his friend he'd talked to half a dozen workers in the kitchen, and every one of them was pissed off big time about the threat to their benefits and pensions. "Old Morton, he's been a cook goin' on thirty-five years, he was looking to retire next year, move down south where he's got property. Now he's scared he'll have to work 'til he's ninety, end up dying on the job."

Lenny had been hearing similar stories all week. "The good thing is, if you can call it good, for the first time I'm hearing the current workers sympathizing with the retirees. They've never been united around an issue before."

"'Bout time they came around, we've been talking about all for one, one for all for years," said Moose. "We need to put out a leaflet, tell everybody to join us on Saturday at the union hall."

"Yeah, but we can't write anything about a march on the hospital, it's got to look spontaneous, remember. Let's talk about it on break, we can meet in the sewing room."

Moose agreed to make it and hurried off to give out trays on Seven North, the sister unit.

<><><>

As the transport orderly pushed a stretcher down to room 705 for Miss Gittens, Mimi went into the room to tell the patient it was time for her test. "Are your dentures out?" she asked.

Gittens reached for her denture cup and shook it. The rattling sound confirmed she had removed her uppers and lowers, as Mimi had instructed her.

"Oh, I'm so glad it's you sending me off, Mimi. You are

always so comforting."

"Well I'm happy to be the one doing it, Miss Gittens."

Mimi helped anchor the stretcher so that the patient could slide over from the bed. As the transport orderly raised the head of the stretcher, Gittens reached out for the nurse's hand in hers.

"Will you pray with me, dear?" said Gittens.

"Of course. You don't mind, do you?" she asked the orderly.

"I never mind somebody calling on the Lord," he said, stepping away from the stretcher. With their hands joined, Gittens and Mimi recited the Lord's Prayer together. Then Mimi pulled the top sheet up to the patient's chin, making it neat and square. She watched the stretcher roll down the hall, hoping her patient would beat the odds and the test would find no cancer.

Anna was thankful for small favors, at least she could walk Maribel to the school bus in the morning. Waving good-bye to her daughter, she walked slowly back toward her apartment building. With no job to go to, she felt lost and listless. She was a nurse: putting on her uniform, going off to the hospital, taking report and caring for her patients — those were the landmarks of her life. She knew that soon the hospital would send her last pay check; how would she survive after that?

She opened the lobby door and held it open for an elderly couple, he walking with a cane, she holding his arm and steadying his gait.

Anna was so preoccupied with her situation, she did not notice the late model car with the darkly tinted windows parked across the street. She could not see Jimmy, who was seated in the driver's seat watching. He had seen Anna walk Maribel to the bus stop. Now he watched her enter her building.

No uniform this morning, he thought. Jimmy wondered if Anna had the night off, or was the story he heard from a friend at the hospital true: was she really in trouble big time?

Was he finally going to get the rights that every father deserved?

9

On the way to the sewing room for his morning break, Lenny saw Regis Devoe coming from the autopsy suite pushing a cart laden with specimens. "Reege!" he called out. "Got a minute?"

The young man turned and looked back at his friend. "Yo, Lenny, what's the union doing about this bull shit cutting our benefits? We gonna kick some ass, occupy the President's office?"

Walking beside Regis, Lenny told him the union was organizing a campaign with a lot of tactics, and it would kick off at the union headquarters at ten on Saturday morning. "But in the meantime I need a favor."

Regis stopped pushing his cart. "Name it," he said.

"You'll be doing the autopsy on the guy they found dead on my floor yesterday, won't you?"

"Yeah, we're doin' it, the M-E gave us the okay. Doc Fingers has it scheduled for four PM today. I hear he was dead for a long time, nobody caught it."

"Maybe not. One of the nurses I work with swears the patient couldn't have been lying in bed dead for hours. She says the night nurse would never make that kind of mistake, so I agreed to snoop around. Not that I can help her much, it sounds like she screwed up, but I'm looking into it."

"Just like old times, count me in. What do ya need?"

"Well, the nurse was wondering if there's any kind of medical condition that could make rigor mortis develop very rapidly. In an hour, say."

"Sure, I can ask Doc Fingers about that, if there's anybody who knows rigor it's him. But they calculate the time of death based on body temperature."

"Did anybody take his temperature after they pronounced him dead?"

Regis thought that wasn't a normal protocol when a cardiac arrest was called in, but he promised to check the records and try to find out if the temperature had been taken. "What else you need?"

Lenny put his hand out to open the door to the sewing room. "A cause of death would be nice, I hear his blood sugar was way low. So low they couldn't count it."

"Too much insulin," said Regis. "It's gotta be from a drug overdose."

"That's the mysterious part, the man wasn't a diabetic."

"You're thinking somebody wanted him dead?"

"Don't go there," said Lenny, raising a single dark eyebrow at Regis, his most serious look. "As far as I know, I'm investigating how the guy could die right before the night shift ended and still be in rigor mortis, and, who could've given him a shot of insulin."

As Regis moved on down the hallway, leaving Lenny at the door to the sewing room, he said, "No worries, brother. But if Doc Fingers finds a gunshot wound to the head, you'll be the first one to know about it."

<><><>

When Mimi heard the dispatcher order her down to Mr. Hatcher's room "STAT," she grasped the GPS unit hanging from a lanyard around her neck and silently cursed, knowing the dispatcher could hear every word she spoke. Since curses were a violation of hospital policy, Mimi and the rest of the nurses had learned to silently mouth their curses or to express them with hand signals that expressed their anger and disgust.

Mr. Hatcher was a chronic complainer.

She knocked on the open door, put on the best smile she could muster, and entered the room.

"Good morning Mister Hatcher," she said. "What can we do for you today?"

"I'm supposed to take my god damned pills with breakfast, not after the meal," he said. "You brought them to me late, as usual, and now my breakfast is ice cold! You need to warm it up or I'll write another letter to the Patient Relations people. Not that they're good for anything, all they do is sit across from my bed and listen."

Mimi suppressed her anger at the old man. Her view of him was softened a bit, knowing he was a widower. But even so, there was no reason for him to curse and write her up, it wasn't her fault she was late with the meds. She'd called down to Pharmacy and asked for a STAT delivery, Hatcher's was a new drug order. But Pharmacy said they had nobody to deliver the meds right away, she'd have to wait for the regularly scheduled drug run, and that wouldn't arrive until nine or nine-thirty at the earliest.

A call to the Messenger Service had been equally fruitless, Mets was swamped with requests to deliver patients, leaving them no time to go for a few pills.

The nurse tried to explain her predicament, but Hatcher wouldn't hear it. He railed about the inefficiency of the institution, the lazy attitudes of the nurses and the brainless pronouncements of the young residents in training.

"Mister Hatcher, I know the doctor said to take your pills with food. You could have eaten your bacon and eggs and saved your toast for when the meds arrived. That would have been fine."

"That's not how I do things! I take my morning pills with my orange juice, then I follow with my meal. That's the right way to take my medicine, you should know that, you're supposed to be a professional nurse. At least your name tag says so."

Mimi looked down at the name tag on her uniform. The letters RN were printed big and bold beneath her name, an initiative from the new hospital administration to enable patients to know the job category of the people caring for them.

Funny thing was, the nurses and aides and transporters and social workers all had big occupation designations on their name tags but the doctors weren't required to have them. Not even the med students.

Well, life was never fair, Mimi had learned that at a young age. She believed God rewarded the righteous with a place beside him in heaven when they died, but here on earth, the wicked prevailed, that's just how it was.

"Would you like me to get you another breakfast, Mister Hatcher? It shouldn't take very long to get it from the cafeteria."

"No! I want you to reheat it!"

Mimi withheld a quiet curse. She knew it was useless to explain to this angry patient that ever since one patient complained she had scalded her tongue on a bowl of soup the nursing staff had overheated in the microwave, the people down in Legal had forbidden nurses from reheating a patient's food, making the patients wait for a new tray when their own had grown cold.

"It's policy, sir, we're not allowed to reheat patient food."

"That's utter stupidity!"

"You're no doubt right, Mister Hatcher, but I'm sorry,

there's nothing else I can do."

She stepped toward the door, remembering how much work she had to do on the rest of her twelve hour shift. "Shall I call for another tray?"

Hatcher sighed deeply and nodded his head. He looked down at the tray of uneaten eggs, bacon, toast, juice and coffee. "It's a sin to waste food, didn't your mother tell you that when you were growing up?"

"She most certainly did, sir. And that it was a sin to curse another person, too."

She hurried out of the room, pleased with herself for getting out one little barb that wouldn't get her written up.

<><><>

Entering the sewing room on his morning break, Lenny found Moose already there chewing on a soft pretzel he dipped into spicy mustard. Gloria Green was sitting next to Moose's wife, Birdie, who was repairing a torn sheet on her big industrial sewing machine.

"Yo, Lenny," said Birdie, looking up from her work. "What's the union gonna do t' keep the hospital cutting off my benefits? They can't do that, can they?"

Lenny opened up a battered metal folding chair and settled into it. "It's more like what are we going to do about it," said Lenny. "The bastards can get away with whatever they want as far as the law in concerned. The benefits contract has a clause that lets them bail on it if the money in the fund drops below a certain level."

"The mother humpers talk like it's our fault our benefits are in trouble," said Gloria. "Like we can't manage our own money. But that's not true, is it, Lenny?"

"The hospital has been underfunding the retirement account for years," said Lenny. "Back in the nineties when the stock market was flying high, the hospital lowered their contribution rate. They said the fund didn't need that much going in, it was growing with the market."

"Yeah, but then the whole fricking stock market collapsed, remember?" said Moose. "We lost a bundle from our fund."

"That's it," said Lenny. "The hospital refused to bring their contribution rates back to what it used to be, and the fund has been struggling to stay solvent ever since."

"Those shit-assed mother humpers," said Gloria. "We got to get the word out on how they're doin' us. Get the people on our side!"

"That's why the union urged all of us to write to the governor and our state representatives. And call in to the radio talk shows. Any way we can put the truth out for the public to hear about."

"What about a big demonstration?" said Birdie. "We gonna march on the hospital on Saturday?"

Lenny explained that the demonstration had to look spontaneous, it couldn't be attributed to the union or they would be in breach of their contract.

"That contract don't mean jack shit!" said Gloria. "Hospital breaks the contract every day. Besides which, they don't want to recognize our union anyway."

"I agree, the hospital is trying to have it both ways," said Lenny. "They can file legal complaints if we take an action not allowed by the contract, and they can turn around and claim they don't even recognize our right to represent the membership."

"So why are we sticking to the contract?" asked Gloria.

"It's on account of we can't ask them to recognize our contract if we tear it up and act any which way we want ourselves," said Moose.

"Man," said Gloria, "these cockapoo laws are totally per-
verted. We got to get us some new laws!"

They agreed to quietly spread the word about meeting
at the union hall Friday. When asked what the purpose of
the meeting was, they would tell the members they trusted
that it was to get everyone together for a march on the hospital. For the members they considered shaky, they would
just say it was for a march to City Hall.

As Lenny and his friends left the sewing room, the security guard monitoring the video cameras made a notation
of the date and time. He would add it to the log of Lenny's
movements, measuring his time away from his work station down to the second.

And building a case to remove him from service.

When Evie left the laundry room for her morning break,
she didn't go to the cafeteria for coffee. Instead, she made
her way to the security office, making sure nobody she
knew saw her turning down the corridor and entering the
office.

The guard at the call center looked up, saw who she
was and gestured with his thumb for her to go on in. Ner-
vous around people in authority, Evie walked toward Joe
West's office trying to not bring any attention to herself. At
West's door she knocked, heard a familiar gruff voice say,
"Enter!"

Joe West, dressed in his habitual crisply pressed, navy
blue suit and silver handcuffs hanging from his belt, looked
up at Evie. Not offering her a seat, he said, "Well?"

Evie cleared her throat, which had constricted as soon as she entered the office. "Mister West, I went to the union meeting, like I told you I would. They're all angry and excited and stuff. They asked us to write letters and call up the politicians and the radio stations and make a lotta noise."

"That's par for the course with those people. It won't save their contract. But what about any actions? Didn't they announce any public displays? Are they coming to the hospital?"

"President Echols said we was marching to City Hall and he was gonna give the politicians a piece of his mind. Raise all kinds of hell and all."

West studied Evie's face, his dead, shark eyes making her even more afraid. "You're sure they didn't say anything about marching on the hospital?"

"Uh-uh."

"Nothing about occupying the administrative wing? Blocking the entrances?"

"No, sir."

West stared at Evie another long minute. Satisfied that she was telling the truth as far as she knew it, he waved her away with his hand and looked down at a file on his desk.

Frozen in place, Evie cleared her throat and said, "Mister West, you still gonna get me into the dialysis tech program, ain't you? You promised me a place in the class."

"Of course I'll get you into the class. You just have to take a test to qualify and you'll be enrolled."

"A test? What kinda test?"

"It's very simple, just some basic English and simple math. A child could pass it blindfolded."

As West turned his attention to a file on his desk, Evie slinked out of the room, fearful about the entrance examination. Math was not her strong suit; her reading and writing skills were not much better.

With the door closed, West opened a file and reviewed the video surveillance pictures of Lenny Moss's movements around the hospital. The time stamps on the pictures told him exactly when he left his work station and when he returned. The sojourns were longer than permitted by the work contract, but not by much. Not enough to terminate him.

He needed more, and he knew just how to get it.

10

Anna Louisa sat in her little kitchen staring at a cold cup of tea on the table. She felt numb and lost. After walking Maribel to the bus stop, she had returned to the apartment and made a cup of tea, which now was cold. "Ah, mi, what am I going to do?" she said to herself.

The silence in the room was interrupted by a knock on the door. It was the postman with the certified letter. She signed for the letter, placed it on the dining room table, and sat down. Staring at the unopened letter, she felt the tears welling up again.

After a long fearful moment, Anna opened the letter. It contained a check. She didn't know if the amount was correct but was too despondent to think about it.

The letter stated that she had been terminated from James Madison Medical Center for unprofessional conduct causing harm to a patient in her charge, and for falsifying documents related to the incident. It went on to say she was not eligible for workman's compensation. It ended by warning her not to visit the hospital except for medical care or she would be arrested for trespassing.

Anna cried as if she would never run out of tears. She called her mother, who lived in Florida. Between sobs she told her mother what had happened in the hospital and how she had been fired. "Mama, what will I do if I lose my nursing license? What if I cannot support me and Maribel? Oh my god, what if they arrest me and Jimmy finds out? The judge will give him custody of Maribel!"

Her mother tried to reassure her daughter, saying they would hire a good lawyer who would make everything all right. "Jimmy is a bad man," she added. "He will never have custody of Maribel. Never!"

"He is very smart, mama. Jimmy can talk sweet. He fools everyone."

"He does not fool me! I see through his big smile and his happy talk." She told Anna she would take the bus tomorrow and come to help her.

"No, mama, you do not need to do that."

"I will come. I will be there day after tomorrow. God is good, He will make all things right. You will see."

Mimi helped the orderly transfer Miss Gittens from the stretcher to her bed. Having heard the report from the nurse in the GI lab, she knew that doctor had found a suspicious mass that was probably cancer. Mimi's heart filled with sorrow for the lady, knowing she was in for some difficult surgery, and almost certainly a rough course of chemotherapy.

Plumping the pillow beneath Miss Gittens' head, Mimi asked how was she feeling.

"My tummy is all swolled up," said Gittens. "It's tight as a drum!"

"That's normal after the procedure. Once you pass more flatus it will go down."

Miss Gittens grabbed Mimi's hand. "Did they find any cancer? My mother died from bowel cancer, I'm so afraid the same thing will happen to me."

Adopting her best poker face, Mimi said, "I didn't see

the procedure results yet, Miss Gittens. I'm sure your doctor will be by soon and answer all your questions. Okay?"

Turning to go, Mimi was interrupted by a long, loud blast from the patient's rectum. She turned and smiled broadly at her patient.

"See? Don't you feel better now?"

Miss Gittens pressed gingerly on her belly and found it softer. "Oh, yes, that feels so much better." With a twinkle in her eye she asked, "Do you think that nice young man could bring me a little breakfast?"

Mimi was taking away Miss Gittens' late breakfast tray when Beatrice reported that Mr. Manwatty had spiked a fever. Hurrying to the room, she found the young man breathing rapidly and sweating profusely. His blood pressure was low and his pulse was high, all signs of septic shock.

"Hi, Mister Manwatty. Not feeling so well today, huh?"

"I feel very bad. I have pains all over my body."

"I'm calling the doctor, we'll get you right as rain before you know it. Hang in there, okay?"

Cursing under her breath so that neither the patient nor the dispatcher could hear, she paged the Hospitalist resident STAT and retrieved a liter of saline solution, anticipating an order to run it into Manwatty's bloodstream. Rapidly.

As soon as the resident heard Mimi's report of the patient's deteriorating condition he gave her the okay for the rapid IV infusion and asked her to draw a blood culture. "I want a full sepsis panel as well," he told her. "And don't forget the lactate level."

"I know the protocol, doctor, thank you. Will you be transferring Mister Manwatty to the ICU?"

"That's up to my Attending, but I'll notify Admissions, I'm sure that's where he'll be going."

As Mimi connected the IV bag and started the infusion, she asked the resident if he would notify ID about the change in condition.

"That's up to Doctor Bilici. But I'm sure ID already knows. "

"What do you mean?" said Mimi.

"Did you enter the vital signs in the computer?"

"Of course, that's the first thing the aide did."

"Then Teepee has already sent an alert to Bilici and Auginello. I suspect they are on their way."

"Lord have mercy," she mumbled leaving the room to ask the aide to rush the blood work to the lab.

Meeting the Hospitalist team outside Mr. Manwatty's room, Dr. Auginello wasted no time making his recommendation. "Start him on TB meds," he said. "I want the full four-drug regimen."

"But the chest X-ray is essentially clear," said Dr. Bilici. "Why the TB meds?"

"He hasn't responded to broad spectrum antibiotics. He's septic. We have to cover all the bases."

Bilici folded his arms across his chest and frowned. "Then why not start anti-fungal treatment?" Opening the computer program, Dr. Bilici pointed out that Teepee listed TB in the "highly unlikely" category. Although the Hospitalist Attending hated to decline a recommendation from the ID service, especially when it came from Dr. Auginello, he didn't like going against the computer patient management program. At the same time, he knew TB drugs could produce profound adverse side effects.

"Michael," Bilici began.

"I know, you'd be sticking your neck out. I don't like it any better than you do, but I've seen disseminated TB before, and it's ugly."

Auginello looked at the Hospitalist resident, who, tasked with inputting all orders, was waiting for his Attending's approval to type in the four drug TB regimen. The resident looked at Dr. Bilici,

"You do know where eighty per cent of all disseminated TB cases are diagnosed, don't you?" said Auginello.

Bilici nodded his head, a glum look on his face. "In the morgue. They usually make the diagnosis on autopsy." The Hospitalist nodded to his resident, freeing him to order the four TB drugs. When the resident ordered the first drug, Rifampin, the computer program rejected it. The young physician pointed at the red flag on the computer screen.

"Override it," said Bilici. "And call the ICU Attending, I want this patient transferred to the unit for close monitoring."

The Resident overrode the blocked order, entering a note in the text box that justified it, then continued with the other three drug orders.

"I hope to hell you're right, Michael. The CMO will have our heads on a platter if we're wrong and Manwatty dies."

"Not on a platter, Galen," Auginello told him, striding off on his long legs. "On pikes! He'll have our heads mounted on pikes!" He left humming the old Scottish song about Loch Lomond.

<><><>

Lenny was wiping down the hand rails along the Seven South corridor when he spotted a beguiling figure coming down the hall pushing an x-ray machine. When the tech reached him, Lenny took his cloth and said, "Can I wipe down your machine, ma'am? I can get it looking all shiny and new for you. Really make it shine."

Patience put her hands on her hips. "Don't you mess with my machine, Lenny, Clarence keeps all our equipment clean and running just fine!" Then she poked him in the stomach, eliciting a grin on her husband's face.

"How's your day?" he asked.

"It's okay. We've got a tech out sick, so you know how that goes."

Lenny understood. He told Patience that after work he was going to visit a nurse who had been fired but he expected to be home in time for dinner. "Are you okay with that? Can you be there to let the kids in?"

"Lenny! Our daughter is old enough to let herself into the house. She can be there when Malcolm comes home."

"I know, it's just ... I worry about them being home alone."

"Why? 'Cause they're gonna get into trouble like you did when you were their age?"

"They better not pull the kind of crap I did back then. No, I worry about some druggie or pervert following them home and getting in the house."

Patience put a hand gently on Lenny's arm. "Do you think I don't worry about them every day I'm at work? But they're growing up, Lenny. We have to give them more independence. If we don't, they'll rebel in a bad way. Give them a little trust, it'll pay off in the end."

"I don't know..."

"And if they mess up we'll ground them and make them take violin lessons."

"Ouch! A fate worse than death." He gave Patience a peck on the cheek and resumed his work, still worried about the children being home alone until Patience arrived, but knowing she was right, he had to give them a little more independence or they would go the other way big time, just as he had done as a child. Sneaking out of the house at midnight and meeting friends to hang out, not doing anything bad, just savoring the peace and quiet of the night and their independence.

Until his dad found his bed empty and was waiting downstairs for him. With a leather belt.

Not that Malcolm and Takia would be home by themselves for that long a time, Patience finished at 3:30. If she got a ride with Birdie she'd be home by 4:00. That left the children home alone for less than an hour. Not that much time for them to get into trouble.

But time enough for somebody else to make trouble for them.

11

Lenny stood outside Anna Louisa's apartment collecting his thoughts. He had stood outside more doorways than he could remember, preparing to meet with a union member in trouble. Too many times the meeting was to deliver bad news: an arbitration hearing had gone against the worker; compensation had turned down a petition; a co-worker had refused to testify on behalf of the terminated worker for fear of reprisals.

This time he felt it was the wildest of goose chases. But Mimi was sharp, she could tell a good worker from a slouch, so there had to be something more to the story.

As the door opened, Lenny felt a familiar pang of sorrow, seeing Anna Louisa with eyes swollen from crying and a face weighed down by sorrow.

And fear.

"Hi," he said. "Mind if I come in, have a word?"

Knowing Lenny's role of union steward, Anna led him into the little living room, decorated with old fashioned oak and embroidered furniture. He figured most of it had been in the family for many years. Settling into an upholstered chair with a sagging seat, Lenny asked how was she doing.

"Oh, I'm okay, I guess," said Anna, "I mean, as good as I can be. It's not easy, losing your job all of a sudden. It's... it's kind of a shock."

"Oh, I know it is," said Lenny. "I've been through it myself. You think your life is stable and predictable. You figure you're going to go to work day after day until it's time to retire, and then out of the blue, bang, you're tossed out into the street with nothing. No benefits. No job prospects. It's hell, it really is."

Anna said, "Would you like some coffee or tea? Or a glass of beer, I have a bottle cold in the refrigerator."

"No, thank you, I just had a cup before I came over."

Anna sat quietly, not saying anything for moment. Lenny had learned from years of union advocacy it was important not to rush someone when they had something difficult to tell him. Waiting and listening were the cornerstone of his steward work.

"I still don't understand what happened," said Anna. "I am sure that I checked on the patient in A-bed at six, like I always do."

"You're sure of the time?"

"It was more like six-fifteen or six-twenty, because I started giving out my six am meds at twenty minutes before the hour. I am sure I did not inject him with insulin. I couldn't have, he was not diabetic, there was no medication order for it!"

"You couldn't have given the wrong patient the shot? Is that possible?"

"I know it could not happen. I don't understand how the insulin bottle could be in Mister Landry's tray when the pharmacy restocked in the morning. It was not there on my shift. And I do not understand how Mimi could find him in rigor mortis when he was sleeping normally at six-fifteen!"

Lenny sat quietly trying to make sense of it all.

"It sounds like there are several mysteries all jumbled together," Lenny said. "First, there's the question of how the insulin bottle got into his medication drawer; second, who gave him the insulin; and the most puzzling part of all to me, how he could go into rigor mortis so quickly."

Anna described looking at the patient's chest and assuring herself it was rising and falling at a normal rate.

"What did he look like exactly?" said Lenny. "Did he look comfortable? Like a normal sleeping person looks?"

"I didn't see his face, he was turned away from the door, I only saw him from the back. I'm sorry! I should have looked more closely."

"No, no, you did your job the way you're supposed to, you have nothing to apologize for. And the patient wasn't due for any medications or you would have had to wake him up."

"Yes, that is so. I had no reason to wake him."

Lenny pictured the scene in his mind. He could not see how the patient could be breathing normally at one moment and then stiff in rigor an hour later. It made no sense.

"The only possible explanation that I can come up with is that the man had some kind of weird disease that made the rigor come on very quickly," he said.

"Is there such a condition?" asked Anna.

"I don't know, I don't have any kind of medical training." He mulled over the problem. "Were any of your patients getting insulin injections?"

"No! Nobody. I had two patients on oral medications for sugar, but none of my patients were getting insulin."

"So there wouldn't have been any injectable bottles in your medication tray." Anna shook her head no. "But it's part of your floor stock, right?

Anna reluctantly nodded her head yes. "You think I am not telling the truth. That's what you think, don't you?"

"No! I believe you, Anna. I just don't have an explanation that fits all the pieces together. A puzzle like this is going to take time to figure out."

Anna smiled for the first time since Lenny arrived, a little encouraged that someone believed her.

"I have heard stories about you, Lenny. About how you help people when they are in trouble. They say you are a miracle worker."

"I'm a long way from that. Mostly I just ask a lot of questions and don't believe most of what people tell me. But I believe you, that's not the issue."

He went on to say that he had asked a friend to tell the pathologist he should take a close look at the body when they did the autopsy. Plus, his friend would ask the doctor if there were any medical conditions that made rigor mortis come on in an hour instead of the usual three to four hours.

Lenny thought about the puzzle some more. "The nurses wear GPS units that track your movements. You were wearing yours that night, weren't you?"

"Of course. It is grounds for termination if we take them off while we are on duty."

"Hmm. If the hospital holds onto the record of your movements, it would show whether or not you stepped into the dead man's room around six in the morning. Right?"

"Yes, it will definitely show I was in the room." Anna's face brightened with new hope.

"Although..." Lenny said.

"Although what?"

"I know how the boss can twist the facts in a hearing. They will say ok, you stepped into the room, but you missed seeing the man was dead and not breathing."

Anna's look of hope withered and died. "Lenny, Mimi says this could be a criminal matter. She says I could be charged with a murder! If I go to jail I am afraid Maribel's father will take her from me, he has gone to court because I don't want him to see her. You have to help me get my job back!"

She went on to explain that her ex-boyfriend was a bad man. "Jimmy can talk sweet and sound nice, but inside he is cold and mean," she said. "He has no heart."

"Does he provide child support?"

"Not like he's supposed to. He used to work as a salesman, but he lost that job. Now I don't know how he makes his money. Maybe he sells drugs, I don't know for sure."

Lenny tried to reassure her that the GPS would still strengthen her case. "What about the nurse's aide who worked with you. Did she take his blood pressure that morning?"

"No, that was taken at ten pm by the three-to-eleven aide. Mister Landry was scheduled for discharge that morning, so I told the aide not to wake the man, they would get it on the day shift." Anna's eyes suddenly welled up with tears as she told him she was afraid she would be arrested and put in jail.

Lenny stood and stepped closer to her. He put a hand on her shoulder. "Try not to think about that for now Anna Louisa. I will do everything I can to keep that from happening. Okay?"

Anna dabbed her eyes with a paper napkin. She rose and led Lenny to the door. At the door he advised her not to talk to the police without a lawyer present. When Anna opened her mouth in horror at the thought of answering questions of the police, he assured her that the police interviewing somebody did not always mean they would be charging her with a crime.

He left her wishing he could promise to make all the problems go away, but he was a union steward, not a magician. He would do what he could, knowing it might not be enough.

Although the information gleaned from the interview was discouraging, Lenny didn't think it was a completely hopeless case. Just ninety-nine per cent hopeless, par for the course in his line of work. He needed to gather a lot more information if he was going to pull some kind of scrawny, half-crazed rabbit out of his union hat.

12

The body of Mr. Landry lay on the stainless steel autopsy table. Wearing a surgical mask, eye shield and a long waterproof apron, Dr. Fingers began a cursory examination of the body while Regis Devoe, the morgue assistant, set out the containers for collecting specimens.

Finding no signs of trauma on the body, the pathologist held his hand out for the circular saw, but then withdrew his hand.

"Why don't you make the initial incision today?" he said.

"You sure, doc?" said Regis.

"I'm sure."

Finger watched the young man slowly and carefully run the blade along the breast bone and then outward at a 45 degree angle toward the shoulder. Regis was doing well, which was no surprise, he was a serious young man. The pathologist recalled the day that Lenny had come to him to recommend Devoe for the morgue assistant position. Old Fred had gone to his Maker; what a tragedy that had been. While the physician initially had doubts about the candidate, given Devoe's long history of work infractions and suspensions, Fingers also knew that Lenny's word was always good. The young man had turned out to be an excellent choice. He worked late whenever asked and was thorough in his tasks, plus, he didn't tell terrible jokes or drink the way Fred used to do.

Once the incision was finished, Dr. Fingers dissected away the anterior rib cage. He spoke into a microphone clipped to his plastic apron, recording his observations as he used a scalpel to cut away connective tissue and nerve fibers. He noted that Landry was a well-nourished Caucasian male, five feet ten inches tall.

With the anterior ribs and breast bone removed, Fingers began to inspect the organs within. The lungs, deflated in the chest and detached from the chest wall, were sagging gray sacks. Dr. Fingers severed their vascular, neurologic and connective tissue connections, removed the lungs and set them on the scale.

"Say, doc," Regis said, receiving the first sections of lung tissue for microscopic examination, "there's something about this autopsy you should know."

"Oh?" said Fingers, looking up from the open chest.

"This guy that died, the nurses are saying there's something suspicious about the death."

"You mean besides the profound hypoglycemia and the possibility of a fatal medication error?"

"Yeah, besides that."

"What kind of suspicious?" Fingers freed the heart from its connections and held it up reverently in his hands, like a priest making a benediction.

"Well, the body was in full rigor when the day nurse found him, but he was breathing normally about an hour before that."

"Impossible. Couldn't happen."

"That's why it's suspicious. The nurse is sure he was breathing an hour before they found him stiff as a board. Lenny told me to ask you if there's any kinda medical condition that can make rigor mortis set in in, like an hour, maybe less."

"Lenny Moss thinks the death is suspicious?" said Fingers. "Why didn't you tell me from the get-go?" The pathologist, who had helped Lenny solve a number of suspicious deaths in the past, told Regis to order additional lab tests on the blood, serum, tissue and extra-cellular fluid he had collected. "What else?"

Screwing down the lid on a specimen cup and pressing a label on it, Regis told the doctor that the nurse was saying she didn't give the patient any insulin, he wasn't diabetic.

"Of course she's going to deny administering a fatal drug, wouldn't you?"

"Prob'ly so, but Lenny says the nurse is a solid professional. She wouldn't do anything that stupid."

"I'll reserve my opinion until all the lab work is back and I've viewed the frozen sections," said Fingers. "I need to review the literature on rigor as well." Dr. Fingers looked at the cadaver with fresh eyes. "If Lenny suspects foul play, I'm leaving no stone unturned. Hand me the magnifying lens, I'm going to look for injection marks."

Smiling beneath his surgical mask, Regis held out the magnifying glass for his boss. Lenny had helped him out of more than a few jams. It felt good to be the one doing the helping for a change.

While Lenny was driving home from his visit to Anna Louisa, the big Buick stalled at a stop light. Lenny turned the key, hoping he wouldn't have to call for a tow. On the third try the engine fired with a mighty roar, sending a puff of black smoke out the exhaust. He knew the rings were bad and would cost a bundle to replace, if his mechanic could find them, the car was, what, twenty years old? Not to mention the brakes. And the muffler.

Patience had reminded him more than once, they needed a reliable car, for the kids as well as for his union organizing. Time to trade it in, though he hated to let it go, it had been his father's car. But Lenny's house had no garage where he could work on it, and car restoration was way too expensive on his family's modest income.

As he drove on, he pictured the patient in 706 sleeping in his bed, soon to be found dead. Did the roommate wake up early and see Landry asleep? Anna hadn't said anything about a patient in the B bed. Lenny made a note to ask Mimi in the morning about that.

Considering a worst case scenario, where Anna had given the patient the insulin injection, Lenny realized the nurse would have discarded the syringe in the sharps container hanging on the wall, the nursing staff were trained not to carry used syringes from room to room. The sharps containers were emptied on Monday and Friday, if they were more than half full, so a potentially damning piece of evidence should still be in the room. He made a mental note to check the container first thing next morning.

Driving along Germantown Ave, Lenny kept the rpms high, even at the traffic stops, worried the next stall would be final. Pulling up to the house in east Mt. Airy, he parked the car facing the wrong way, a Philadelphia tradition, and ambled up to the porch, knowing Patience was right, as usual, it was time to trade in the car for a newer model.

Seeing a red alert flag pop up on his cell phone, Dr. Roger Slocum repaired to his office, where he poured two fingers of scotch into a crystal glass. He opened Teepee on his computer, which displayed Manwatty's deteriorating vital signs, having earlier added his name to the list of physicians who were consulting on Mr. Manwatty. The program sent text alerts to his cell phone when any abnormal vital signs or diagnostic test results were entered into the system.

Slocum wanted to be certain he was winning the wager with Auginello, the victory would help solidify ADTP's dominance over the physicians, the prelude to layoffs and trimming the staff. He saw that the patient's blood pressure had dropped and his heart rate gone up. A repeat blood test showed a rising lactate level, a sign of impending septic shock. Sipping the whiskey — a just reward for his challenging day — Slocum nodded approval on seeing the order for three liters of normal saline to be infused rapidly, knowing that under-treating septic shock was the primary reason that too many patients died from sepsis in the hospital.

But when the CMO saw that Dr. Bilici had added four TB meds to the treatment regimen, he became alarmed. ADTP did not recommend treatment for tuberculosis, the chest X-Ray was essentially normal. Scrolling through the patient history, Slocum saw that the patient had received a TB vaccine in childhood. Although TB vaccination was not a highly effective preventive measure, still, it decreased the likelihood that the patient was suffering from tuberculosis.

"Christ almighty!" he swore to himself. The chest x-ray was essentially negative. There was no cavitary lesion. What the hell was the Hospitalist thinking?

Slocum paged Dr. Bilici STAT. Before the Hospitalist could even say hello on the phone, Slocum was chewing him out for treating Manwatty for tuberculosis.

"TB is down at the bottom of Teepee's differential! You should be looking at toxic shock! Candidemia! SBE. What the hell are you doing over there?"

Bilici told Slocum that the echocardiogram had been negative, ruling out infection of the endocardium, and bacterial antigens had also come back negative. Fungal smears likewise were unremarkable.

"Your chance of seeing fungal clusters in a blood specimen are almost zero," said Slocum. "The computer put candidemia in the differential as likely, just below bacteremia. Why are you adding TB drugs? It makes no sense!"

Bilici reminded the CMO that most patients who developed disseminated tuberculosis were only diagnosed on autopsy. "Doctor Auginello didn't want this young man to be another post mortem surprise. He felt it was better to err on the side of caution than miss the diagnosis and have to explain to the family why we failed to initiate the appropriate treatment."

Slocum told Bilici to start the patient on anti-fungal drugs STAT. He reminded the Hospitalist that if the patient died and they found no TB on autopsy, he would have both physicians' heads on a platter, then he slammed the phone down.

Speaking into a dead phone, Bilici mumbled, "Don't you mean, our heads nailed on a stake?"

13

Settling into a comfortable chair in his study after a leisurely dinner with his wife, Dr. Fingers sliced off the tip a Cuban cigar with an old scalpel no longer sharp enough to handle tough connective tissue, scratched a wooden match on the side of his desk, and drew on the stogie, purchased on a trip to Canada. He was looking forward to being able to buy them in the US, once the new trade agreements were implemented. The physician thought he and his wife might even take a trip to Havana, he'd wanted to visit the country for a long time.

Taking up a thick, heavy pathology text book, he opened it to the section on rigor mortis, leaned back, set the cigar in the ashtray, and read the entire chapter. He asked himself if rigor could present with an onset of less than an hour after death. He couldn't recall such a case in his twenty-odd years working in the pathology department. Fingers read on, noting that a prolonged period of profound hypotension with septic shock altered the intra-cellular levels of calcium in muscle cells. But the chapter did not suggest that full rigor could be significantly accelerated.

The only relevant finding he could find in the textbook was a footnote that stated exposure to extreme cold temperatures at the time of death could lock the muscles and give the appearance of rigor mortis. But the patient in room 706 had been lying in a warm hospital bed, there was no possibility of chilling the body at the point of death. What's more, the false rigor only lasted a short time.

He studied the physical findings associated with profound hypoglycemia, since the death was likely due to the insulin overdose. The text said nothing about low blood sugar accelerating the onset of rigor.

Finishing with the chapter, the doctor relit his cigar and went online to begin a wider search of the medical literature.

Piling an extra pillow at the head of the bed, Lenny told Patience about his interview of Anna Louisa. His wife shook her head in disbelief.

"Of course she checked on her patient. The bosses always blame a worker when something goes wrong. Like the time they found radiation oncology was using too high a level of radiation and burning the tissues. They blamed the techs but it was the machine that was faulty. Remember?"

"I remember. We had to take that grievance to arbitration, it took almost two years to settle it."

She handed him a bottle of lotion. "Do my back? My skin is so dry!"

He poured a healthy dollop and lowered the straps of her nightgown. "You have sexy shoulders."

"I have boney shoulders, I never could keep much weight on."

"You need to eat beef. And pork. And lamb, lamb is very healthy."

"I'll stick with my grains and vegetables, thank you." She started to laugh. "All that meat you eat hasn't kept you from going bald, you know."

"I'm not going bald, I just have this one spot on the back of my head."

"Yes, but it's growing bigger every day. You should shave your head. You'd look very sexy with a shaved head. And a little goatee on your chin."

"No goatee for me!"

Finishing with the lotion, he kissed her neck gently while she raised the straps on her nightgown.

"We need to go away for a while," said Patience. "Don't you think?"

"The kids are in school."

"I mean without the kids. My aunt can watch them for a few days."

"We'll have to hide the liquor."

She jabbed him in the chest.

"Ouch! That hurt!"

"So did your smart ass remark. Lorraine drinks less than you do."

Lenny had no answer for that remark. He pointed out the union was in heavy negotiations with the administration over the threat to stop paying into the workers' health and pension fund. She said they could go away after the contract was signed.

"You're always busy with the union issues. I'm not complaining. But you need some time to relax and get away. We both do."

Agreeing to start looking for a place they could drive to, Lenny told Patience about the car stalling out again. He promised to go with her to shop for a new car: not a brand new one, but something considerably newer than twenty years.

"What about a little convertible?" Patience said.

Lenny picked up a copy of the Daily News and opened it to the sports section. "Too easy to break in to." In a terrible foreign accent he added, "I beg of you, be on guard. This place is full of vultures, vultures everywhere."

"Huh." Patience opened a magazine and blocked sight of her husband. She was not amused by his Casablanca reference.

<><><>

Dr. Fingers was immersed in an online article about rigor mortis and sepsis when he heard a light rap on the open door. Looking up, he saw his wife standing in the doorway, a troubled look on her face.

"Problem, dear?" he asked.

"Uh, Nelson, there's a police detective at the door. He says he needs to talk to you about a wrongful death at the hospital."

"Ah, yes, I've been expecting him. Send him in." Closing the computer program and turning off the computer, Fingers called to his wife, "And would you put on a pot of coffee? This may take some time."

The pathologist took out his box of Cuban cigars to offer the detective.

14

After punching in at the hated time clock, Lenny sat in the housekeeping locker room donning his black steel-toed work shoes when his friend Abrahm sat down beside him. The Russian fellow removed his shoes and set them down on the bench.

"Jesus Christ," said Lenny, "are those the same shoes you wore when you first started working in this dump?"

"Yes, Len'nye, they are the same. They are vury good shoes."

"How many times have you replaced the soles?"

"Only three times. Why should I buy new shoes when only the soles have worn out?" Abrahm tucked the shoes gently in his locker, put on his steel-tipped work shoes and held the door open for his friend as they went out to their work stations.

Lenny arrived on Seven-south a half hour before his shift began. He wanted to look over the room where Mr. Landry had died. Not that he expected to find anything useful, the death had occurred two days ago. The rooms were thoroughly cleaned after a discharge, so the old linen and personal effects would be long gone.

He saw Maddy, the aide on the midnight shift, emptying urine from a patient's Foley bag. Following her into the bathroom where the aide would discard the urine, he asked if she had a moment to talk.

"You wanna know about that poor Mister Landry that up and died, don't you?" Maddy said.

Lenny shook his head in wonder. "How come everyone knows my business even before I do? Mimi had Anna Louisa's phone number and address written out for me even before I knew anything about the man dying."

"You got a rep, Lenny, ain't no use tryin' to run away from it." Maddy rinsed out the container she had carried the urine in and set it to dry on a rack. Washing her hands, she asked what did Lenny want to know?

"Well, Anna told me she saw the patient was sleeping comfortably a little after six am. Nothing seemed wrong with him. Did you see him that morning?"

"Uh-uh, I didn't even go in the room. Anna told me they could get his vital signs on the day shift, he was scheduled for discharge, I should let the man sleep."

"So you didn't go in the room at all?"

"Nope. The patient never put his call light on, so I had no reason to go in."

"You didn't walk past his bed to check on the patient in the B bed by the window."

"Na-ah, that room was empty all night long. We were thanking our lucky stars we didn't get no admission that night. Must've been a slow night in the ER."

As Maddy was about to leave the soiled utility room, she asked Lenny if the union was going to kick the boss's ass to hell and back on Saturday.

"We will if enough workers show up for the rally."

"I'll be there for sure," said Maddy. "Ain't nobody taking away my benefits, my husband needs a new hip! Think I can pay for that outta my own pocket?"

Lenny considered Mimi's comment that Mr. Landry had died from an insulin injection. Since the nurses were instructed to discard their syringes in the sharps container on the wall and not to carry it out of the room, then Anna would probably have dropped it in the sharps container the room.

Going to room 706, Lenny was surprised to find the A bed empty and made up ready for a new patient. The curtain was pulled back, exposing the patient in the B bed.

"They transferred the man to the ICU last night," said the patient in the bed by the window. "Poor fellow wasn't doing too good. I hope they turn things around, he's a polite young man."

"I hope so, too," said Lenny. He saw that the sheets on the bed were taut and folded in the traditional hospital bed fashion, the over-bed table set parallel to the side rail. The furniture was clean and polished.

He peered into the narrow throat of the sharps container hanging on the wall. There were only a few syringes lying in the bottom of the barrel. None of them were the slim ones with the tiny needle used for insulin, they were all bigger ones. That was disappointing, the fatal syringe might have the killer's fingerprints on it.

Lenny stood a moment staring at the bed. If Anna had stepped into the room not long after six in the morning, she had to have seen that Mr. Landry was breathing normally. The only reasonable explanation for Mimi finding him in rigor mortis an hour later had to be some weird medical condition that brought on the condition quickly. Nothing else made sense. Unless the man wasn't breathing normally and Anna failed to check on the patient.

Or if she killed him.

Cursing under his breath at the intractable problem, Lenny went to the housekeeping closet to set up his equipment for the morning, hoping that when he got the GPS tracking record for Anna's nursing rounds it would confirm her story, and hoping that Regis would bring him some kind of useful news about this mysterious rigor mortis.

<><><>

Nurse Gary Tuttle entered Mr. Manwatty's hourly vital signs in the computer program, including the patient's hourly urine output. He noted the clear, yellow color of the urine, which was free of sediment. Gary always looked to a patient's urinary output as a sign of how well he was doing, it was a poor man's measure of cardiac output, since it directly reflected perfusion of the kidneys.

"You feel like taking a little breakfast?" he asked.

"Perhaps a little tea," said Manwatty. "And could I trouble you for a little lemon and sugar? If it's not too much trouble."

"No trouble at all," said the nurse. "I saved some lemon slices from yesterday, they should be in the fridge."

Returning with the cup of tea, Gary was pleased to see Dr. Auginello and his Infectious Disease team clustered around Manwatty's bedside, accompanied by the ICU Attending, Dr. Fahim. While serving the tea, the nurse reported the patient's status to the doctors.

"Are you drawing lactate levels every four hours?" Auginello asked. "I want to follow the lactic acid trend." Gary confirmed the night nurse had sent off a specimen and he already had the labels printed for the follow-up test, knowing lactate was a good indicator of the degree of sepsis and shock.

Auginello noted the blood gas results were not encouraging. "His A-a gradient is too high," he told Gary. "You better send off blood gases every four hours along with the lactate level."

The ICU resident entered the order in the computer.

"Should we continue the TB meds this morning, Doctor

Fahim?" the resident said, all medical decisions in the unit being up to the ICU Attending.

Dr. Fahim rubbed his belly, having not enjoyed his usual egg and toast breakfast this morning.

"Michael, you know that Teepee put TB at the bottom of the differential."

"I'm aware of that," said Auginello.

"I accept your argument that disseminated TB is usually discovered on autopsy. But we can't rely on the usual antibody test, the patient was apparently vaccinated for TB, it would be a false positive. Not only that, but because tuberculosis is exceedingly slow to grow on culture, we will not have any culture results for several days."

"Which is all the more reason to treat for TB early and not wait for confirmation from Microbiology," said Auginello.

Fahim's eyes, usually bright and laughing, were dark. He hated to go against the opinion of the ID division, especially when Auginello was on service. But they were bucking the new computerized program, and it did utilize the most advanced diagnostic algorithms.

Leading the team away from the bed so the patient would not hear, Fahim said, "I know about your wager with Slocum."

"My decisions are based only on my best clinical judgement."

"Of course, I don't doubt that. And I am happy to take your side, Slocum is a toady for that smug bastard Reichart. He wants to replace physicians with his computer program, it's ridiculous. But I remain concerned about the side effects, these TB drugs are nothing to fool around with."

"Samir, I realize going against Teepee can be dangerous to a physician's career at James Madison."

"That means nothing to me whatsoever!" said Fahim, his eyes flashing with anger. "A computer will never replace the insight of an experienced doctor!"

Auginello waited for Fahim to make up his mind. Finally, the ICU Attending agreed to keep the patient on the TB meds for at least another 48 hours.

"Look on the bright side, Samir if I'm wrong, we face the music together."

"Yes, the music together. And the lawsuit!"

Lenny was wiping down a discharge bed in a private room, lifting the mattress to get to the frame and platform beneath. Sometimes patients bled or discharged various fluids that ran over the edge of the mattress and soiled the hard surfaces beneath.

Satisfied the entire bed was clean, he stepped out to the corridor for his mop and bucket when Mimi saw him.

"Okay if I make up that bed now, Lenny?" she said. "I got an admission coming from the Family Medicine clinic."

"Yeah, I'll help you make up the bed and then I'll bring an admission kit and mop the floor."

As Mimi spread a fresh fitted sheet over the mattress and pulled it over the corners, she said, "It smells nice and fresh."

"I add a little bleach to the soap solution. Not too much or it'll take out the color, just enough to kill more bacteria."

Mimi pulled the bottom sheet taut, then she spread the top sheet over the bed. "How are you doing with, you know, the thing?" she asked.

Lenny focused his eyes on the GPS device hanging on a strap around the nurse's neck.

"A nurse I talked to recently told me how they track your movements throughout the hospital," he said.

"They sure do. We like to joke the dispatcher can tell if we're doing number one or number two in the toilet from the sounds we make."

"Christ, that's gross." He eyed the device. Leaning in close to her, he whispered, "Any way to turn it off?"

"Battery," Mimi whispered, turning the unit over and snapping off the back. She pulled the battery out and looked at Lenny. "Did you talk to my girl last night?"

Lenny knew from years of reporting to workers on his negotiations with the boss, when he had to deliver bad news, the straight story, gently expressed, was almost always the best approach.

"Yeah, I met with Anna Louisa last night. She seems like a good person. Solid. Reliable. At least that was my impression, the little time I spent with her."

"That's what I've been saying, Anna is a good nurse."

"I'm sure. She's worried the nursing board is going to pull her license."

"Mother Burgess loves to report our nurses to the board. It's not enough to fire a nurse and get her a bad reference, she's got to stick the knife in and twist it, too."

"Like too many bosses, I'm afraid," said Lenny. "How is Anna going to earn a living?"

"I have a good friend working at a nursing home out in Norristown. I think I can get her a part-time job out there, but she'll have to work weekend nights."

"That sucks, it's a big drop in pay."

"Tell me about it. At least it will keep her from losing her apartment and having to live in a shelter with Maribel. That would really hurt her in court."

"The custody fight. Yeah, she told me about it. That's a rough road." Lenny began mopping the floor. "I checked the sharps container in seven-o-six, I was hoping I'd find the insulin syringe that was used on Mister Landry. Maybe have the perpetrator's fingerprints on it, but it wasn't there."

"You could've asked me, I already looked. And it's not in the little sharps box on my medication cart, that was the first place I looked when I heard about the insulin overdose." She leaned in close and whispered, "I heard security came and confiscated both the sharps containers, took them down to Joe West."

"Shit. I should have thought of this right away." He set the CAUTION WET FLOOR sign up. "Well, if there is an answer to this mystery, I don't see it." He saw Mimi's face sink. "I mean, I believe Anna's telling the truth. I just don't have any alternative explanation other than the one that Miss Burgess came up with." He studied the nurse's face. "Do you?"

"No, but that just means we haven't looked in the right places yet."

"Speaking of places, I was saying to Anna Louisa, they must keep a computer record of your movements on that GPS unit. Right?"

"Of course. Last month they wrote up Larissa for being down the cafeteria past her twenty minute break. We think the time it takes to get to the cafeteria and to get back to the ward shouldn't be counted as break time, but Mother Burgess won't hear about it."

"We get the same crap. I was thinking, the GPS log will show if Anna went into room seven-o-six at six am, as she says she did."

"That's right, it will! But you better believe the administration won't give that to you. They never admit when they screwed up. Never."

"That's okay, I have a friend in IT. I'm pretty sure he can access the server where the GPS records are kept."

As Mimi opened her mouth to speak, Lenny held up a hand to silence her. "The thing you have to know, Mimi, is the records might show Anna never went into the room. And if they do show she went in, that wouldn't prove she observed the patient alive and breathing normally."

Mimi's face switched from hopeful to worried again.

"Too bad the patient wasn't hooked up to telemetry," said Lenny. "That would have solved everything."

"No such luck, Mister Landry was ready for discharge. The aide didn't have to get six am vital signs."

Lenny peeked out into the hallway to be doubly sure no one could hear them. "I think I can get a copy of Landry's chart, can you get all his lab results for me?" When Mimi told him that was easy to do, Lenny cautioned her to not use her own login.

She winked at him, saying, "Mama didn't raise no fools," and returned the battery to its proper place, while Lenny went on with his duties.

15

Dr. Winslow Greene sat with Miss Gittens. A large man with soft hands, he sported a bow tie and a warm smile.

"It's not good news, Miss Gittens, I won't try to minimize it. The pathologist confirmed you have a malignant tumor invading your transverse colon." He paused to let the news sink in, watching for a reaction.

The patient reminded her physician that her mother and her aunt had both died from cancer, she had been expecting the disease to come for her one day.

"Believe me, a diagnosis of cancer is not the end of life. We have to do more tests to determine if the cancer has spread. And there are new genetic tests that will tell us a lot more about the degree of malignancy and how best to treat it."

Gittens sat quietly, her hands folded in her lap, a picture of stoicism.

Dr. Greene took her small hand between his large, soft hands and held it, like a blessing. Fighting an impulse to kiss her hand, a gesture inappropriate to the occasion, he gave her a gentle squeeze. "I'm not giving up on you, young lady. I want you to be clear about that."

"Thank you, doctor. I know you have my best interests at heart. But you see, we both know what is coming, don't we?"

The doctor's heart filled with compassion for his patient. He tried to reassure her that the new DNA tests could help them design the most effective chemotherapy agents; that in her mother's era chemotherapy was administered blindly, it was hit or miss.

Seeing no sign of optimism in Miss Gittens, the doctor released the patient's hand. He touched the top of her head, wishing he could instill some kind of healing energy, but knowing there was no magic in medicine.

Not when the diagnosis was cancer.

On his mid-morning break, Lenny hurried down to the IT department hoping to find his friend Damien. Sure enough, he spotted the top of the man's bald head in his cubicle. Damien was typing on his keyboard faster than anyone Lenny had ever seen.

"Yo, Big D, how's life in the virtual world?"

Damien's hands froze for a second, then resumed their blistering pace as soon as the IT tech realized it was not his supervisor calling out to him. Finishing, he hit the send button, pushed his rolling chair back away from his desk and leaned back in his chair, arms outstretched to his friend.

"Lenny Moss, the man, the myth, the legend. To what or to whom do I owe the honor of your visiting the land of the black arts?"

Lenny shook both his friend's hands, a custom he never understood but went along with. "Hi, Damien. How've you been?"

"I've been grand, just grand. We're applying a new security patch on the mainframe and it is rocking."

"Glad to hear it. Listen, I have a delicate sort of problem I need help with. It's not exactly kosher. If you got caught..."

"Say no more. I haven't forgotten how you helped my niece Valery when she was working down the laundry during that bad heat wave. You got them to run the machines at night when it was cooler. And to dry the clothes without all the heat."

"Yeah, that was a tough fight. So, can we talk in here?"

"I have jammed all of Joe West's surveillance devices in our department, and everybody's out on assignment or getting high. What can I do?"

Lenny explained the issue with Anna Lisa's claim that she went into a certain room at six am to check on a patient, but the administration was claiming she never entered the room.

"Ah, yes, that poor sod the day nurse discovered in rigor. Sounds like another lawsuit for old James Madison."

"They track the nurses on their GPS devices, don't they?"

"Indeed they do, my friend, much to my chagrin and regret. I hated to hear when they announced the new monitoring program, but as a lowly prol toiling in the digital bowels of the hospital there was nothing I could do about it."

"Well, can you retrieve the records and get me a print out?"

"Does a bear shit in the woods? Is the Pope Jewish? Of course I can retrieve the data. It will require a day's wait and a bottle of bourbon?"

"Rebel Yell?

"Pul-eeze. I am a Bulleit man. Don't you recall?"

"Yeah, okay, I'll bring you a bottle tomorrow. After you give me the print out."

"The deal is done. You will join me on the morrow for a drink, then."

"If I can, I'm crazy busy with the union campaign, but

we'll see."

Lenny left, buoyed by his friend's willingness to break into the hospital computer records and help him out. He only hoped the information would put the nurse in the dead man's room at six am.

As Lenny hurried back to his work station, he noticed a security guard standing down the hall from the IT department. Didn't I just see that guy on the Seventh floor?

<><><>

Slipping into the staff lounge, Mimi called Anna to tell her about a possible job in a nursing home out in Norristown. "It won't be permanent, you'd just be getting some shifts until you get your job back at James Madison."

"Do you really think they'll take me back? Miss Burgess is so mean. You should have seen her when she told me I was fired, it was like she enjoyed it."

"Don't worry about her, that friend I sent over to see you yesterday? He's real good at solving problems. He'll figure out what really happened to Mister Landry, and then you'll be back on Seven-South before you know it."

"I pray every night for help, Mimi, and so does my daughter. I am so scared I will be arrested and her father will take Maribel away from me, ay dios mio, it keeps me up at night worrying, worrying. What will happen if I go to jail?

"I know you're afraid, Anna, but believe me, when my friend sinks his teeth into something, he doesn't let go until he's got it licked."

Saying good-bye, Mimi slipped out of the lounge and returned to her duties. She knew the dispatcher could have listened in to her conversation, which is why she didn't mention Lenny by name. What Mimi didn't know is the dispatcher had instructions from Joe West to listen to and record any conversations related to the death of Mr. Landry.

Which is why the dispatcher called the security office and told them he had a recording of the phone conversation. When a security guard came to the dispatch room and asked for the tape, the dispatcher asked him, "Isn't it illegal to record somebody's conversation without telling them? I mean, isn't that why they have to tell you, 'This conversation may be recorded for quality purposes.' Right?"

The guard assured the dispatcher that employers had the right to listen to and record any conversations made while on the job.

"But the nurse didn't use a hospital phone, she was on her own cell."

"Makes no difference," said the guard. "She was on duty, there's no expectation of privacy."

The guard held out his hand. After a few seconds' hesitation the dispatcher handed over a cassette with the recording.

"I just hope nobody finds out we're recording what people say," said the dispatcher.

"No worries, it's all for quality control."

16

After mopping the floor for the new admission, Lenny spied Moose coming down the corridor pushing the lunch cart. As Moose pulled two trays out at the first room and carried them in to the patients, Lenny joined him.

"Have you heard the latest brain storm from Personnel?" asked Lenny,

"No, what're they cooking up this time?" Moose pulled out two more trays.

"They're talking about making the custodial staff help with the food trays."

"Brilliant," said Moose. "After you clean a bunch of toilets and mop up a pool of diarrhea, you're the perfect guy to handle food."

"I don't think they'll get very far, the union has already sent a complaint to the Department of Health about it. But they might order us to pick up dirty trays."

"Heh, heh. They wanna keep the staff from picking over the leftovers. Who's gonna take half a ham sandwich from a tray after you handled it?"

"I certainly wouldn't eat it," said Lenny. He waited for his friend to serve another pair of lunch trays. "Say, Moose, your cousin still work in Medical Records?"

"Tiffany. Yeah, she's still there."

"Think she'll do you another favor?"

Moose thought a minute. "Well, they're serving chicken cordon bleu for a reception today, that's Tiff's favorite... Yeah, I think she'll help me out. You want a copy of the dead guy's chart, I'm guessing,"

"That's it."

"Have it for you by the end of the shift."

"Great. Let's meet at the Cave after dinner and see what we've got."

Lenny returned to his duties, emptying trash liners in the patient rooms, and marveling that there were workers in the hospital who would put their jobs in jeopardy to help out a nurse who had been wrongfully terminated. Solidarity forever.

Nurse Gary Tuttle emptied an hour's worth of urine from a metered container into the larger collecting bag hanging from Manwatty's bed. It was still clear and amber, a positive sign. The patient's vital signs were unchanged, with a heart rate of one-ten. Fast, but not yet dangerously so.

As he recorded the amount in the twenty-four flow sheet, something in the back of his mind nagged at him. It had something to do with the urine, but he couldn't put his finger on it. The output was adequate, the color was good, but some obscure medical fact was dancing around in his brain somewhere. If he could just grab it and hold it down long enough to know whether it was trivial or important.

Gary withdrew the four TB meds and the IV antibiotic from the medication cabinet. He hung the IV, then raised the head of the bed enough to make it easier for the patient to swallow the tablets.

"One of them's a big one," said Gary. "Take your time with it."

Manwatty took the fat pill in his mouth, raised the glass

of water to his lips and took a long draught.

"Got it down?"

The patient gave him a thumbs up, then he sank back into the bed, exhausted by the simple effort of swallowing four pills and a few ounces of water.

<><><>

Dr. Fingers was staring into a microscope at a slice of cerebral cortex when Regis came in with fresh specimens from the GI Lab.

"Say, doc," Regis said.

"Hmmm?" Fingers said, not looking up from the microscope.

"You get anywhere with that question about rigor setting in kind o' quick like?"

Fingers looked up and turned to Regis. "As a matter of fact, I did find one exception to the expected timeline for the onset of rigor mortis. It seems that if you chill a body rapidly right at the time of death, it can induce a muscle rigidity that resembles rigor, although it has a different clinical presentation."

"Yeah, but how's a patient in a hospital bed gonna be chilled? From what I hear, his body wasn't ice cold when they tried CPR on the guy."

Fingers brought his eyes back to the microscope. "I'm afraid that's the only exception I was able to find in the literature. Oh, you may find this interesting." Fingers made a notation about the slide he had been viewing on a tablet computer. "I found no puncture marks on the cadaver's skin."

"So the insulin..."

"Had not been given by injection. Which can only mean..."

"He got it through his intravenous line right into the blood."

While Fingers removed the slide and set another one under the lens, Regis sent Lenny a text saying they should meet up after work.

"Say hello to Lenny," Fingers said, putting a grin on his assistant's face.

After serving all the lunch trays on the seventh floor, Moose returned to the kitchen, where one of the chefs was setting stuffed chicken breasts on a platter and garnishing them with sprigs of parsley.

"Hey, Donnie. I need a piece for a friend. You okay with that?"

"Okay by me, just don't let the dietician see it, she'll tell the boss."

Moose set on a tray a plate of chicken cordon bleu, mashed potatoes with gravy, cornbread and a bowl filled with bread pudding. He covered the tray with a towel.

Donnie winked at Moose. "Who's the girl you trying to sweeten up?"

Moose said, "Never you mind, it's for Lenny, he's trying to get somebody their job back. Ain't nothin' in it for me."

"Yeah, sure."

Making his way to Medical Records, Moose found Tiffany in her cubicle. Pictures of two young children, a little dog with a black button nose, and a handsome man in a fireman's uniform were tacked to one of the cubicle walks.

Tiffany saw the tray, grinned widely, then frowned. She squinted as she looked up at Moose.

"What you need this time, coz?"

"Heh, heh. I know how much you like chef's chicken cordon bleu. Brought you a double helping."

He lifted the towel from the tray. She sniffed the exquisite aromas.

"Times like this I wished I'd married a man who loves to cook like Birdie did."

"What're you talking about? Stanley makes the best ribs in all 'o Philly, and he's got the awards to prove it."

"Yeah, but he can't scramble an egg without leaving pieces of the shell behind." She placed the towel back over the tray. "I'll take this down the break room, we're not supposed to eat at our desks. Now, I s'pose you're here about that poor Mister Landry. The death that got the nurse on Seven South fired."

"How'd you know I was here about that?"

"C'mon, Moose, I know you and Lenny are like salt 'n pepper shakers on a lunch counter. The man died on his ward and the nurse worked there, too. O' course you two are going to take the case." She turned to a filing cabinet and pulled out a folder. "The police already asked for a copy of Mister Landry's chart. I printed everything out this morning."

Moose stood open-mouthed in the middle of Tiffany's cubicle.

"Don't look so surprised, Moose, it's not like this is the first time you asked for a chart." She promised to copy the medical records and have them waiting for him when his shift ended.

Moose left amazed and impressed at his cousin's smarts and her guts. That Stanley is one lucky man, he thought.

17

Dr. Roger Slocum sat across from Robert Reichart's desk trying not to squirm as his boss typed on his computer, ignoring the Chief Medical Officer. Slocum thought, why do I feel like a grade school kid called to the principal's office every time he summons me? Not one for serious introspection, Slocum put the question out of his mind and looked at the pictures on the wall. When he saw the photograph of General George Patton hanging there, he recalled that Reichart had served in the US Marines and been a Green Beret. Slocum wondered why the CEO didn't have a picture of Napoleon up there, too. He waited in silence, knowing that engaging the CEO in light banter was worse than crapping in his pants.

After a moment, Reichart looked up from his desk, almost as if he had been unaware the Chief Medical Officer had been seated before him.

"I am not pleased with your wager over the outcome of the patient Manwatty," said Reichart. "Wagering on a patient outcome could bring negative publicity to the hospital if it ever got out."

"It wasn't a serious bet, it was more a joke than anything else," said Slocum.

"Demanding that Doctor Auginello buy your department dinner is not a joke, I'm surprised you would consider it a matter of levity."

"I just mean—"

"Never mind!" snapped Reichart, raising a hand to stop

Slocum in mid-sentence. "I want you to tell the ID Attending that the wager is off. You will tell him in person. Today."

Slocum nodded his head yes, not trusting his voice.

"I understand that ADTP puts tuberculosis at the bottom of the diagnostic tree, is that right?"

"Yes. The computer ranks it very low probability."

"Then have you objected to the Hospitalist Service agreeing to the TB treatment?"

Slocum squirmed in his chair. "It is difficult, Mister Reichart, to go against the medical decision of an Attending physician unless you have very good literature behind you. Especially when ID made the recommendation."

"The computer has already reviewed the relevant research findings. Your doctors have got to get that clear in their minds: the program does the search and analysis for them. All they have to do is follow the recommendations."

"Of course. I've explained all that. It's just, sometimes a physician will go on a hunch. Or on their own clinical experience, which may not have been written up in the literature."

"Which is precisely why they have to get on board."

Reichart warned Slocum that if he could not get more of the Attending physicians on board with the program he would find someone else to take the CMO position, then he dismissed Slocum with a curt wave of his hand.

Dr. Slocum left the office yearning for a drink and wondering how in the hell Reichart knew about the wager he'd made with Dr. Auginello. He must have spies and snitches all over the facility.

<> <> <>

As Detective Joseph Williams climbed the stairs to the apartment on the fourth floor, he was glad he'd gone back to working out at the local gym. Having torn the medial meniscus in his knee and undergone two months of physical therapy, he decided to join a local gym. He soon expanded the lower body exercises the therapist had taught him and added an upper body workout, along with thirty minutes on the treadmill. Not that climbing the stairs today left him eager to take up stair climbing for exercise.

Williams withdrew his police identification and knocked on the door. After a moment the tiny peephole window in the door brightened with light. He held his ID up for the occupant to see.

"Philadelphia police department, can I come in?"

He heard the chain being withdrawn and the lock turned. The door opened.

"Are you Anna Louisa Mendoza?

Anna nodded her head.

"Can I come in? I need to ask you some questions."

Trembling with fear, Anna looked down at the floor as she stepped aside to let the detective pass, then closed the door and followed him into the small living room.

Williams looked at a chair.

"Please, sit down," said Anna.

She took a seat on the sofa beside him, clasping her hands in her lap and again looking down at the floor.

Taking out a pocket notebook, he said, "I have to ask you some questions about the death of Mister Otis Landry. He was your patient the night that he died, is that right?"

Anna nodded her head yes.

"Can you tell me what happened?"

Anna continued to not look into the detective's face. Her throat was constricted and her heart beat so hard in her chest she thought it would burst through her ribs.

"Miss Mendoza, this is difficult for you, I understand. But I have to gather the facts in order to make sense of what happened. You can understand that, can't you?"

Anna again nodded her head yes.

"Why don't you start from the beginning? Of your shift, I mean."

Anna looked toward the ceiling as if seeking guidance or reassurance from heaven. She swallowed, then began her story. Anna told Detective Williams how she had checked on Mr. Landry every hour of her twelve hour shift, and that he had been breathing normally a little after six when she made her last round.

"I did not give my patient any insulin," she added. "No way, it was not in doctor's orders. I would not do that. Never."

When Williams pointed out that a bottle of insulin was discovered in the dead man's medication cart, Anna declared it had not been there during her shift.

The detective asked if the victim had had any visitors during her shift or if there had been anyone on the ward who did not belong there. Anna admitted she had not seen anyone who was not supposed to be there all night.

He asked where she had worked before taking a job at James Madison Hospital and if she had ever been licensed in another state. Anna had heard stories about nurses who lost their license to practice in one state after making a major medical error and gone on to practice in another, so she was sure the detective wanted to check on her record. She told him she had attended nursing school at Philadelphia Community College and had always worked in the Philadelphia area.

"And you have no doubt that you saw the patient breathing normally on your last rounds?"

"Yes! Yes, I am sure I did, he was sleeping peacefully."

"Then how do you explain the day nurse finding him in full rigor not more than an hour later?"

Anna's throat was so contracted she could barely croak her reply. "I cannot explain it."

"What about the insulin? We know Landry died from an insulin injection he wasn't supposed to receive. And there was a bottle of insulin n his medication drawer. How do you explain that, Miss Mendoza?"

Unable to hold back her tears, Anna hid her face in her hands and cried. "I don't know! I should not talk to you, that is what my friend told me. Do not talk to the police if you don't have a lawyer with you."

"What friend?" said Williams.

"Somebody from work."

Detective Williams saw a box of tissues nearby, handed her a few. He never knew what to say to a woman in tears. The detective understood that Anna might hide her true feelings behind a fit of crying, but he didn't think she was pretending. Guilty or innocent, she was frightened.

"Did the dead man have a roommate? Somebody who saw you go and check on Landry?"

Anna shook her head no.

Seeing he could get little more of value from Anna, Detective Williams pocketed his notebook, stood up and thanked her for answering his questions. As she opened the door for him, she wanted to ask if he was going to come back and arrest her, but the question was too terrifying to put into words.

Williams was about to leave when he stopped and turned back to face Anna.

"By any chance, was this friend who advised you about a lawyer Lenny Moss?"

Anna sniffled and nodded her head yes. In no way surprised, the detective left without further comment. Having traded information with Moss during more investigations than he wanted to remember, Williams knew who he would next have to talk to. He chuckled as he pictured the unimpressive figure in his blue custodian uniform mopping the floor — the perfect disguise for a razor sharp private detective.

Anna collapsed onto the sofa, too numb to cry any more, too afraid to think. Not knowing what her fate would be was the worst part of the nightmare that plagued her waking hours and haunted her sleep. She didn't think all the prayers and the candles in the church would protect her from going to jail, or keep Maribel from going to live with her father.

18

Anna Louisa and Maribel were just coming out of the ice cream shop, each licking an ice cream cone dripping on their hands. When a car abruptly pulled up beside them, its windows dark and impenetrable. The passenger window started to lower.

"Maribela, how's my best girl?"

Taking her mother's hand, Maribel looked up at her, not sure if she should speak to her father.

"Jimmy, you have to stay away from us! I have a court order!"

"That judge don't mean nothin' to me. I hear about your troubles. I know you got no job."

"I will find another job! You will see."

"I don't think so," said Jimmy. He held his arms out, the wrists close together as though they were in handcuffs. "Who gonna hire a woman killed her patient? No-body!"

Anna squeezed her daughter's hand and led her away from the street, a shiver of fear running through her. She trembled to think what would happen to her daughter if Jimmy had sole custody, especially once she reached her twelfth birthday and became a woman.

"I will be with you soon, my best girl!" he said with a laugh. Jimmy raised the passenger window and sped away, the tires of his car squealing on the pavement.

When Maribel looked up at her mother, she did not see the face of a calm, confident professional woman. She saw fear and despair.

The melting ice cream ran down over the girl's hand and onto the sidewalk.

Lenny was hanging up his mop and getting ready to go punch out at the time clock when his cell phone vibrated. A new text message from Damien, his friend in the IT department read, "Kitty caught a mouse." The message had a file attached. It was Anna Louisa's GPS record the night of Landry's death.

Though anxious to know what the GPS record showed, he decided not to open the file until he was out of the hospital, there was no telling how far Joe West would go to spy on him. The ever present security guard who was dogging his movements confirmed Lenny's fears that he was under heavy surveillance. At home he would dump the attached file into his computer and print it out. Lenny hoped the GPS record would support Anna's story. He didn't want to contemplate the consequences if it showed she hadn't stepped into the dead man's room on her last round.

Before leaving Seven South he asked Mimi if she could join him at The Cave when her shift was over. Happy to meet him, she asked if he had good news to report.

Lenny looked at the GPS hanging from Mimi's neck. "Tell you at The Cave."

Mimi mouthed a silent "Okay" and went back to her work, while Lenny wondered just how much the dispatcher heard on that wretched GPS unit.

<><><>

Sitting around a pitcher of beer and shots of bourbon in the Cave, Regis told Lenny, Moose, Gloria and Mimi what he knew of Landry's post mortem. "For sure the man died from an insulin overdose, we couldn't even measure the blood sugar level, it was so low." He added that the pathologist had examined the body with a magnifying glass looking for puncture marks and found none.

"What's that tell you?" asked Moose.

"It means the insulin was given right into the blood," said Mimi. "By the intravenous route."

"Do you give insulin that way?" Lenny asked.

"We do when the patient's blood sugar is really high and we need to bring it down fast. Mostly we give it sub-q: injected under the skin."

"Hmm. How fast does the insulin work when you give it right in the blood?" said Lenny.

"It's, like, fifteen minutes, but it would take a while to drop the blood sugar so low you start showing symptoms. Why?"

Lenny said he was trying to figure out what time the lethal dose of insulin had been given. If rigor mortis took roughly three hours to set in, the insulin would have been given around four in the morning.

"Except it couldn't have been given that early," said Mimi. "Anna saw him breathing on her five and six o'clock rounds!"

Regis added that Dr. Fingers had researched rigor mortis and there was no medical evidence that rigor could set in in under an hour. Mimi said there had to be an exception, but Lenny pointed out that the pathologist was the expert.

Regis went on to say that the only case of fast rigor mortis Dr. Fingers could find was when somebody chilled the body right after death. "But how you gonna chill a body lying in a hospital bed? It don't make no sense."

Unable to solve the riddle of the rigor mortis, Lenny told them how he'd examined the sharps container looking for an insulin syringe but didn't find any. Mimi told them a security guard took away that container along with the one on her medication cart.

"They're looking for the killer's fingerprints," said Regis. Lenny acknowledged that had been his hope in searching the container.

"Sure looks to me like somebody wanted him dead," said Gloria. "We're dealing with a cold son of a bitch."

"Jesus H Christ," said Lenny. "I didn't want to even think this was a case of murder. I kept telling myself somebody accidentally gave the patient an overdose. But now..."

Everyone took up their drinks and contemplated the new territory they were navigating.

"You got to believe it wasn't any accident," said Moose. "Some sick bastard killed Mister Landry and it's up to us to find out who did it. It's the only way to get Anna Louisa her job back. And keep her from being arrested."

"That's something I don't get," said Gloria. "How could the police ever think a nurse would kill one her patients? She's got no reason to murder anybody, she's a nurse. Nurses don't kill their patients."

"Actually, some of the time they do," Mimi said. She explained that in nursing school she heard a lecture about medical serial killers. When the killer was a hospital employee, it was almost always a nurse. "They put the patient into a cardiac arrest so they could start the code and 'save' their life. They want the praise from their coworkers for saving somebody. It's totally sick."

"That doesn't sound like Anna," said Lenny. "She didn't

try to revive the patient. She didn't even know he was dead."

"No, Anna definitely does not fit the serial killer profile. Besides, almost all of the serial killer nurses are men."

"Ain't that just like a man," said Gloria, raising her glass to Mimi, "always trying to pump himself up."

"Exactly. The frail male ego."

Ignoring the women's remarks, Lenny asked Moose if he had a chance to ask his contact in Medical Records for Landry's chart.

"Heh, heh." Moose reached into a battered leather messenger bag, came up with a manila envelope, and handed it to Lenny. "Maybe you can find some reason why the dead man stiffened up so quick in this."

Taking her cue, Mimi reached into a large purse and came up with a printout of Landry's lab work. When Lenny pointed out he needed somebody with a medical background to go over all the material, all eyes turned to Mimi. As the nurse reached out for the copy of the chart, Lenny reminded her she could get in big trouble for receiving the confidential material.

"I know all about the hospital's privacy rules," she said, grabbing the packet out of Lenny's hands. "If the hospital can listen in to all my conversations at work, not to mention any sound I make on the fricking toilet, I'm damn sure not gonna worry about reading the chart of a patient that I took care of."

While Mimi looked over the lab results and chart, Lenny took out his cell phone and opened the file with Anna's GPS record that his IT friend had sent him. He scrolled through the file. "Well at least we have one piece of good news." He showed the others Anna's log. It recorded her entering room 706 at 6.20 on the morning that Landry died.

"So the man couldn't have been dead for hours," said

Regis.

"I agree, he couldn't," said Lenny. "But don't forget how the hospital can spin the evidence. They could claim the nurse went into the room but she totally missed that the patient was dead. After she already killed him with the insulin."

"Never gonna happen, Anna wouldn't hurt a fly!" said Mimi. She raised her shot glass and swallowed the last of her whiskey. "Any fool knows, you go into a patient room, you look at the patient. I do it any time I go in a room, even if it's just to deliver some linen or pick up a lunch tray."

"I agree it would make no sense, but in my experience representing workers, that's how the hospital is going to play it."

"Lawyers," said Regis, downing his shot of bourbon. He sat back and contemplated the mystery.

Moose held his pint of beer between his two big hands, thinking. "Ya know, if Doc Fingers is right and there's no such condition as fast rigor, your girl's got to be wrong about seeing him alive at six twenty."

Lenny said, "I won't give up on her, she seems an honest person. I can't believe she lied to me about what happened."

"But you gotta accept medical facts," said Regis. "Unless Doc Fingers finds some new cases in the literature, the man had to have been dead for three, four hours."

"Speaking of dead," said Lenny, "our union is gonna be DOA if we can't get a good turnout for the rally on Saturday. What have you been hearing?"

Gloria said one of the women in the laundry was not going to go out and demonstrate, she was looking to get a job out in the suburbs, but the rest of them were solid. "They remember that summer the boss made 'em all work in the middle of the heat wave, and how you got them to move the laundering to the midnight shift when it was cooler."

"Yeah, and you kept the heat off on the driers," said Mimi. "We were cheering when we heard about that. I remember, we had to go to paper sheets sometimes, but mostly the laundry kept the supplies up real good."

"They remember what the union did for us down the laundry, Lenny. We're all gonna be out in the street with you."

Moose said the kitchen workers were on board as well. "Soon as you tell a man you killing his pension and dropping his health insurance, that brother is hotter than the oil we fry up our chicken in."

Regis reported he had canvassed the workers in pathology, as well as the diagnostic labs. "All solid," he said. "Hundred per cent."

Promising to bring flyers in to work to promote the demonstration, Moose offered to give them out when he picked up the food trays.

"We have to be careful," said Lenny. "A security guard has been watching me wherever I go. They might be watching the rest of us."

Regis agreed, they had to stay out of sight. "I got an idea how we can get out the flyers." He explained how they could distribute the union literature without being caught. Everyone thought the plan was a good one, with Moose offering to buy the props to make it work.

Lenny brightened with the report. He told them housekeeping was also strong. The aides and clerks, he couldn't speak for, but from what he'd been told, there was strong support there as well. And the retirees were up in arms about the threat to their survival. "Most of the older members will be there, even if they have to stumble along with a walker or drag an oxygen tank."

"So we gonna occupy the administration offices?" asked

Regis.

Lenny looked at his friends. "You think the rank and file is ready for it?"

"They scared of losing their job," said Gloria. "Bad as it is, it's still a union job. The pay's better than most places, an' you got somebody to stand up for you when they try to play their games. Like working over forty without overtime."

"Yup. Or not paying you nothin' at all for stayin' over a couple of hours to finish cleaning up the cafeteria," said Moose. "The only thing worrying me, a lot of our people are pretty old, they're not ready to risk getting arrested, going to court, losing their jobs. That's a lot to ask."

"Nobody loses their job if we all stick together!" Regis made a fist and held it in front of her face. "We all go in and sit down, then we demand no punishment for anybody or we stay 'til the cows come home!"

They kicked different ideas around some more. In the end they decided to march in front of the hospital and give out leaflets to all who came and went. A core group would go into the cafeteria and make a speech to the workers there. Lenny pointed out they could be arrested for trespassing, they would be on hospital property when not on duty, so they would have to restrict their protest to the cafeteria, which was open to the public. Then they would gauge the mood of the workers and decide if they should risk it and march on the President's office.

Draining the last of his beer, Lenny said, "Remember, this will not be a union sanctioned event. The meeting at the union hall, okay, that's official, but when we march on the hospital, that's spontaneous. Right?"

Getting up from her chair, Mimi said, "I'll look over the chart some more, but I don't think it will make a difference, the man died from an insulin injection, there's no getting past that."

Lenny said he would try to learn something about Landry. "Maybe he was mobbed up. Or sold drugs. Something to explain why he was killed."

On that sour note they put their money down and went on home.

19

Tired and a little tipsy, Lenny parked his car across the street from his house and ambled toward the front door. As he reached for his keys, he saw a familiar if unwanted figure standing in front of him.

"I wonder what would happen if I administered a breathalyzer test," said Williams.

"Detectives don't carry those kits, they're too high falutin for such mundane offenses."

"How've you been, Moss?" the detective said, extending a hand.

"Fine until I saw you. You know what time I get up in the morning to go to work?"

"This won't take long. Mind if I come in?"

Lenny shrugged, unlocked the door and let Williams in. After telling Patience about their unexpected guest and looking in on Malcolm and Takia, Lenny joined Williams in the living room.

"Can I get you something? Coffee? A beer?"

"No, thanks, I'm good." Williams took out his notebook and thumbed through it, apparently in no hurry to begin.

"I talked with Anna Louisa today. You gave her good advice about not talking to me unless she had a lawyer present."

"Did she refuse to talk to you?"

"No, but it was still good advice."

Lenny leaned back in his chair and stifled a yawn. He wanted to climb the stairs, crawl into bed and fall asleep with his arm around his wife, but sleep seemed a long way off. The wait made him cross.

"Listen," said Lenny. "How about we cut out the crap and get down to the nitty-gritty. You want to know what I've found out about how Landry died, I want to know what you found out about the victim."

"That's what I like about you, Lenny, no bull shit, no wasted time." He leaned forward, gave Lenny his earnest face. "What have you got?"

Lenny weighed the situation. He had plenty of information. Unfortunately, much of it was illegally obtained, a fact the detective couldn't possibly miss. At the same time, Williams had access to sources Lenny couldn't reach.

"Tell you what. I'll talk a little on a hypothetical basis, you'll tell me what you've learned about the victim. Who he was, if he had any criminal associations, that kind of thing. Agreed?"

"Agreed."

"Okay." Lenny took a minute to consider how to frame his information so it wasn't obvious how he obtained it. "First off, the nurses all wear GPS units around their neck. A dispatcher tells them when a patient needs assistance or a doctor needs help with a patient."

"And the hospital tracks their movements."

"Exactly. They know exactly where every nurse is at any given minute. And, they keep records of the nurse's travels."

"Welcome to the brave new world."

"Tell me about it. Anyway, I suspect that if you got a copy of Anna's GPS record for the morning that Landry died, you will find she did go into his room on her last rounds, say, a little after six am, as well as on her five o'clock and her four o'clock ones, which means she had to see him breathing normally."

"You have a copy of the print out, I suppose."

"As I said, I suspect it will verify her account of the morning in question."

Williams let the issue of Lenny's ill-gotten information drop and asked about the insulin.

"The pathologist didn't find any needle marks in the skin, so the insulin wasn't given by injection. If Anna had given an insulin injection to the wrong patient, there would be a mark on his skin."

"You know this how?"

"I have a friend in pathology." He saw a skeptical look on the detective's face. "It rules out the nurse giving an accidental overdose!"

"I read the autopsy report and I talked with the pathologist, Doctor Fingers. They found traces of insulin in Landry's intravenous catheter. The nurse could have given it that way."

"I'm told nurses only give insulin that way when a patient's blood sugar is like sky high. Landry's blood sugar before the code was always normal."

The detective didn't bother to ask Lenny how he knew the dead man's lab reports, the wily steward had friends in every department, which was what made him such a valuable source of information. Williams pointed out that if Anna had intended to murder Landry, injecting the insulin directly into the blood stream was the most efficient way to do it.

"But that's exactly what proves Anna is innocent," said Lenny. He explained that nurses who were serial killers didn't do it for kicks, they caused a cardiac arrest in order to bring the patient back to life and look like a saint. "Anna didn't try to revive Landry, she didn't even know he was dead."

"Yes, but—"

"Did you look for a pattern of cardiac arrests when Anna was on duty?"

Williams admitted there was no record of the nurse being at the center of any unexpected deaths or heroic resuscitation efforts.

They sat in silence for a moment. Now it was the detective's turn to mull over how much to tell Lenny. He was sure the wily shop steward was holding back information. But without crucial information of his own to offer, he doubted he could get much more out of him.

"About Landry," said Williams. "He didn't seem to have any criminal associations. He was a manager in a clothing store in Chestnut Hill. His boss tells me there was nothing out of the ordinary in his work."

"Did he have access to customer credit cards? Maybe he was involved in identity theft, something like that."

"Well if he was his bank records don't show any unexplained income. No safety deposit box, either, and no big ticket cash purchases."

"No drug use. Gambling addiction. Hiring hookers?"

"Not that I've been able to uncover. We'll keep digging."

"Do you have any idea why somebody would want to kill this guy?"

"None," said Williams.

The two sat for a minute contemplating their mutual failure to make any sense of the death.

"You know what puzzles me the most?" said Williams.

"The rigor mortis."

"That's it. If, as you 'suggested', the GPS does show that the nurse went into Landry's room around six in the morning, I can't see how he could have been alive at that moment and in full rigor an hour or so later."

Lenny told Williams about how chilling a body right after death caused a condition that looked like rigor mortis, but it didn't last very long. Williams didn't find the information useful.

"Even if the nurse didn't administer the insulin, she's still guilty of failing to check on her patient. He was dead and she missed it when she entered the room."

"I'm not buying it," said Lenny. "Anna's not that kind of nurse."

"Alright, then give me a theory that explains the rigor."

"I can't. Yet. Give me some time, I'll have something for you."

Williams got up, shook Lenny's hand, told him to give him any new information he came up with. "I know it's useless to tell you to stop breaking the law. Just be careful."

"My hands are clean."

Lenny closed the door behind Williams and locked it. Exhausted, he stumbled up the stairs, where he found Malcolm sitting on the floor of his room playing with a pair of action figures.

"Why aren't you asleep?"

"I wanted to know what you talked about with the policeman."

"Were you listening from the top of the stairs again?"

"Uh huh."

Lenny kissed the child's forehead. "Go to sleep and stop playing detective."

Malcolm scooted beneath the covers at the foot of the bed and crawled upward until his head emerged onto the pillow. Lenny pulled the sheet up to his chin and quietly stepped out of the room, wishing he was a kid again and not fighting bosses or chasing criminals.

20

When Gary Tuttle began his shift, the report from the night nurse raised his worries about Mr. Manwatty. The patient's condition had deteriorated, with his blood pressure falling, despite the addition of an epinephrine infusion. Even worse, the young man was becoming delirious, a sign that the sepsis shock was altering his brain chemistry. His early morning lab results confirmed the clinical picture, the patient was in the early stages of septic shock.

Gary hung a fresh liter of IV solution to run in fast, hoping to raise Manwatty's blood pressure. After setting the pump, he emptied the urine in the hourly container into the larger collecting bag attached to it. Gary took small comfort that the kidneys were still working; still producing a nice clear, yellow urine, though he knew if the septic shock persisted, the kidneys would soon shut down.

As he entered the volume of urine into his hourly record in the computer, Gary suddenly stopped. There was something about that urine that still nagged at him, but he couldn't capture it. He couldn't identify the little medical factoid that was playing hard to get in his mind.

When he spotted Dr. Auginello coming to the nursing station with a glum look on his face, his team equally glum looking, the nurse knew the doctor had already seen the labs and the deteriorating vital signs.

"Don't be afraid to pour in the fluids," the physician told him. "You keep on running it as long as the blood pressure is low. I don't care how far ahead he is in his I&O, I want his pressure up."

Gary showed Auginello the current IV solution and rate of infusion.

Just then Dr. Fahim joined them at the bedside. This morning there was no sparkle in the ICU Attending's eyes. "Michael, I have a bad feeling about this case, he is showing signs of sepsis. If TB was the cause he would be improving, not getting worse."

Admitting Fahim might be right, Auginello pointed out the patient's air hunger: how Manwatty was opening his mouth as he took in a breath, like a fish pulled out of the water. "His A-gradient is concerning. So is his lactate level. You may have to intubate."

Fahim plucked the stethoscope from around the neck of one of his residents. As he put the ear pieces in his ears, Auginello pulled an alcohol pad from his lab coat pocket, tore it open and handed Fahim the moist pad.

"Oops. Sorry," said the ICU Attending. He rubbed the diaphragm of the stethoscope with the alcohol, then pressed it to the patient's chest and listened.

"There is fluid collecting in his lungs. He is third spacing."

"Until his blood pressure improves I don't think diuretics are prudent."

"I agree," said Fahim. He instructed the respiratory therapist who accompanied him on rounds to put the patient on external ventilatory support. "With a little luck the patient will improve and we can spare him the intubation."

"Gary, be sure to report any drop in his urine output," Auginello added. "I want to save his kidneys at all cost."

Gary's eyes fell on the urometer hanging from the side of the bed with its level of amber urine. All of a sudden that little medical factoid that had been eluding him came into focus. "Doctor Auginello, shouldn't the urine be orange?"

After staring for a long minute at the urine bag, the physician smacked himself in the back of his head. "I am a consummate ass," he said. Turning to his ID team, he asked, "Why should the urine be orange in this patient?"

"Uh, because of renal failure?" asked the intern.

"It is because of the Rifampin," said the ID Fellow. "When it clears the kidneys, it carries an orange pigment with it."

"So, does that mean his kidneys aren't working?" asked the intern.

Instead of answering the question, the ID Attending turned to the nurse for the answer. Gary said, "It means he isn't absorbing the drug from his GI tract."

"Dumping syndrome," Auginello said. "And if the patient is not absorbing the Rifampin, the chances are he isn't absorbing the other TB meds. Which is why his condition continues to deteriorate."

When the ICU Attending heard Gary point out the wrong color of the urine, Fahim said, "This is completely my error. I should have picked that up when I assessed the patient the night he arrived in my unit."

"We're all responsible," said Auginello. "It's a good lesson for the house staff."

Fahim told Gary to draw serum levels for the four TB antibiotics and send them STAT to the lab. "We must determine if the patient's increasing sepsis is because we have selected the wrong antibiotics or if they are not being absorbed," he explained to the House staff and students.

Conferring with the ID team, Fahim ordered three intravenous antibiotics to replace the patient's oral regimen. Gary called the pharmacy to personally tell them the intravenous drugs had to be sent to the ICU by messenger STAT.

Stepping away from the bedside, Auginello told Fahim

that Dr. Slocum had called off their wager. "It was stupid of me to agree to it. It wasn't professional."

"Ah, you took up a challenge, nothing unprofessional about that, Michael. You were defending the integrity of the medical profession against the computer program that is undermining our authority."

"Well, at least we will be spared any more grief from Roger Slocum about it," said Auginello.

"Bet or no bet, it still matters that you beat the machine, Michael. We are counting on you."

"We are counting? Who do you mean?"

Fahim's eyes twinkled with his old mischievous grin. He moved on to another patient without answering Auginello's question, leaving the ID physician to ponder his friend's puzzling comment.

Alone with his patient, Gary Tuttle explained to Mr. Manwatty they would be putting a different kind of mask on him that might be a little uncomfortable, but the extra oxygen would make his breathing easier. Manwatty held up a hand with a thumb up and managed to muster weak smile. Gary read the smile as a positive sign.

Optimism was one of his few character flaws.

Lenny started his day with the buffing machine. The old marble floors were badly in need of cleaning, with multiple ugly brown stains of what, he wasn't quite sure, that required scraping with a putty knife. Before Croesus took over the hospital, the night housekeepers had been responsible for buffing and waxing the floors, since that was the time of the least floor traffic. But with the new company instituting all the cutbacks, the night staff barely had time enough to empty the garbage and mop up the myriad spills of blood, vomit and stool that marred the marble surface, so Lenny got out the buffer when he had time.

The rhythm of the buffer was always soothing for Lenny, it gave him time to think. Remembering the day before, when he'd spotted the same security guard outside the IT department who had also been on Seven-south, he decided to be more careful wandering away from his assigned unit.

Standing outside room 706, he glanced into the room, trying to imagine Anna Louisa's last rounds at six in the morning. The room would have been dark, but still have the night light on. Landry would be sleeping.

The GPS record definitely showed that the nurse had gone into the room shortly after six. The A-bed was the one closest to the door, so even in the dim light, she would have had to be practically blind to miss that he was dead. Stone cold dead. And that didn't take into account her 5 and 4 am rounds, the GPS record showed her stepping into the room at those hours as well.

It made no sense. But he had spent years investigating everything from a patient's missing dentures to tracking down the culprit who left a contaminated spinal needle in bed linen, putting the housekeepers and the laundry workers at risk of being stuck and exposed to one of the many deadly pathogens circulating in the blood. Lenny had learned that all mysteries had a solution, if only he could look around all the corners and catch a glimpse of the truth before it slipped out of sight.

"You figure out who killed Mister Landry yet?"

Startled, Lenny shut off the machine and turned to Mimi, who was standing behind him. About to speak, he hesitated, not wanting the dispatcher to overhear their conversation. That was when he realized Mimi had spoken awfully candidly. And in a loud voice, to boot.

He peered at her neck, saw that the hated GPS unit was not hanging around there.

"I left the squawk box on my med cart. I can hear the dispatcher from here if he calls me."

Lenny told the nurse what he had learned from his talk with the detective: the police had found no sign Landry had been into any criminal activities. He had no debts to a loan shark or bookie as far as they could tell so far. "He was a pretty squeaky clean guy, apparently. He was a manager in a shop in Chestnut Hill."

Seeing Mimi's disappointment, he added that they still might find something that would explain why the man had been murdered.

"I can't figure why somebody would kill a patient in the hospital. Aren't there better places to do it? I mean, look at the risk of being seen."

Lenny reminded her of the housekeeper who had been fired but managed to actually live in the hospital for months, escaping capture, even with the whole security force and all the security cameras looking for him.

"Yeah, that was super embarrassing for Joe West, wasn't it?" said Mimi.

Turning to go back to her medication cart, Mimi stopped and said, "That damn rigor mortis. That's what really bothers me. I found him, he was stiff as a board. If we don't figure this thing out, they're going to arrest Anna, aren't they?"

"It looks that way."

"That means her ex will get custody of Maribel. It's crazy!"

Lenny admitted Anna was probably going to be charged with the crime, possibly negligent homicide, since she had no apparent motive to kill anyone.

"You aren't giving up on my girl, are you, Lenny?"

Promising to keep on digging, he switched the buffer back on with Mimi's parting words echoing in his mind. It certainly seemed like an insane situation. If Anna had seen Landry alive at around six-fifteen, it made no sense that Mimi found him an hour later in full rigor. But those were the facts. It was up to him to find out how.

And why.

He asked himself, *why do I let myself get talked into these fricking investigations?*

Another mystery awaiting a solution.

21

Anna held Maribel's hand tightly as they walked to the bus stop. With so much weighing on her, she had nothing to say in reply to her daughter's chattering away. There was her lost job; she didn't believe the nursing home in Norristown would hire her when they learned she had been fired, even if the head nurse was a friend of Mimi's. And there was the likelihood she would soon be arrested. Lenny said it could happen, and he was a very smart man.

But the worst possibility of all was that Jimmy could get Maribel. Anna hoped her mother could convince the judge to give her custody, but a father's right was strong, how could she fight that? Jimmy had lost his salesman job, it was true, but he was a smooth talker, a good bull shitter, and he had not been arrested. He had not been accused of murder.

Anna looked at her watch, hoping the bus would be along soon. She looked up the street, knowing the direction the noisy yellow vehicle would be coming from.

"Mama," Maribel said.

"Hmm?"

"There is a girl in my class, she does not like the lunch her mother gives her, so sometimes I give her mine. Do you think that is a good thing for me to do?"

"Does the girl give you her lunch?"

"Si, mama."

"And you eat the lunch her mother sends?"

"No, usually I do not eat it, it is not very good. Usually

it is just tuna fish, but it smells funny and the bread is very dry. It falls apart when I pick it up."

Anna could not help but smile at her daughter's kindness, exchanging a good sandwich for one made with stale bread and old fish. She was so like her mother, and Anna was just like her own mama, always giving to help someone in need. Always praying for the souls of the sick and the dying.

As the bus approached belching a cloud of smoke, Anna bent down and kissed the top of Maribel's head. "Tomorrow I will pack two sandwiches for you, daughter!"

"And two cupcakes!" the girl called back, stepping up into the bus, the doors closing behind her.

As the bus pulled away in a cloud of smelly smoke, Anna said a silent prayer of thanks that her daughter was safely on her way to school, where Jimmy was unlikely to go. He had never taken much interest in his daughter's education. Never changed her diapers or sat up with the child when she was sick. Jimmy could smooth talk a customer out of his money, but he had no time for children, he liked grown up girls. That was what finally drove Ann to leave him, the other girls.

Anna trembled to wonder how many more times she would see Maribel off to school before the police took her away to a jail cell.

Walking slowly back to her apartment building, with no job to go to, Anna had nothing to fill her day, except for the fear growing inside her. Fear for her daughter. Fear for herself.

She decided to go to church and attend mass. Turning toward the church, she did not notice Jimmy seated in his car with the dark windows, on a side street a block from the bus stop. Nor did Anna see the car pull out and follow the yellow bus around the corner and out of sight.

When Moose came through the ward to pick up the breakfast trays he told Lenny he had the flyers waiting in the sewing room for distribution. "Birdie's got 'em hidden good. Even if Security comes looking around they won't find nothin'."

Lenny asked about the props, did he have enough to do the job. Moose assured him everything was ready. "That guard still shadowing you?" he asked.

Lenny told him he hadn't seen him that morning but he was sure they were still watching. He pointed to a new security camera set in the ceiling in front of the Seven south nursing station. "They installed that one last night."

Moose retrieved two trays and carried them toward the cart. "We're gonna mess with Joe West's head for sure this time. We'll rendezvous in the sewing room at o-nine-thirty."

"O-nine-thirty?" said Lenny. "What is this, an episode of NCIS?" He watched Moose continue on his rounds, chuckling all the way. For once Lenny was finding no joy in the impending union action, even though it promised to be a major embarrassment for his nemesis, Joe West. There was too much at stake this time; the odds were too high against them.

<>‹>‹>

At nine-thirty am Lenny told the charge nurse he was

going on a break and walked down the stairs to the basement. The heavy footfalls of a security guard following two flights above told him West was still having him watched.

Stepping into the sewing room, he found Moose and Regis already there, along with three male co-workers from housekeeping and two men from dietary. They were all donning gray hoodies. Moose threw a hoodie to Lenny, who pulled it down over his head.

Everyone scooped up bundles of the flyer calling on all union members to come to the union hall Saturday morning and join the demonstration. The flyer read SAVE our benefits - SAVE our lives! It called on all workers to bring their family to the union hall. The flyer said they would be marching down Broad Street to City Hall to demand that the City Council support the workers' benefits and pensions. The union was sending a message to all the hospital owners they couldn't rob the union of the benefits they had won in their contract.

As Lenny reached for a handful of flyers, Moose grabbed his arm and stopped him.

"Not this time, man. This time you go out clean."

"Yeah, but—"

"Ain't no if's, and's or but's about it, Lenny. You know West has security following you. If they do figure out which one of us is you, it don't make no sense you having the evidence on you. Better they search you and come up with squat."

Cursing, even though he knew his friend was right, Lenny joined the other hooded workers filing out of the sewing room. They walked past the security camera in front of the Central Stores department, keeping their heads turned away from the camera, and quickly dispersed in different directions and to different floors.

In the security office, the guard assigned to keep watch

on Lenny looked in horror at the black and white video screen. Although the custodians all wore navy blue shirts and pants, the black and white image, grainy at best, did not allow him to pick out one grade of worker from another. And with the faces hidden by the identical hoodies, there was no way to know which one of them was Lenny Moss.

Panicking, the guard picked up his walkie-talkie and called out to the other officers. "Control to field! Control to field! I need eyes on employees with hoodies coming up from the basement. Find Lenny Moss. One of them is Moss and I can't tell who it is!"

A minute later Joe West burst into the office. "What in the name of Christ is going on? Can't you keep track of one stinking employee?"

"I'm sorry sir, they all were wearing hoodies. And they kept their faces turned away from the camera! I couldn't tell which one was Moss or where the man went off to."

"Play me the video!"

The officer rolled back the time on the video to before the men came down the hall. West watched the gaggle of hooded figures saunter past, unable to determine which one was Lenny.

"So you're telling me Moss could be anywhere," said West.

"Yes sir, I'm afraid so."

West grabbed the walkie-talkie and yelled into it, "Luther! Have you got Moss in sight?"

"That's a negative, sir, I couldn't tell which one was him when they came down the hall."

"I don't want to hear any more excuses. Find Moss! Get me Lenny Moss!"

22

When Lenny returned to his ward, having discarded the hoodie, the guard who had lost him approached the wily steward and demanded to inspect his housekeeping closet. The guard overturned all the containers and searched every shelf, but found no union flyers.

"Be sure to check my locker downstairs," said Lenny.

"Already been there," said the guard, who walked off the ward before reporting on his walkie-talkie that he found no incriminating documents in the shop steward's work area.

Once the other hooded workers dispersed, they returned to their departments, removed the disguise, and began leaving flyers all over the hospital. Dietary workers carried them in their food carts and beneath their late trays. Custodians left them in staff lounges and bathrooms. Laundry workers left them with loads of fresh linen.

By the time the lunch trays had been collected, most of the hospital had been visited. Flyers were taped on walls, in locker rooms and even in the elevators. Security found some, but not before hundreds of workers had seen them. Workers in every department found their hopes rising that their health benefits and pensions would be saved.

Although disappointed that he had not been able to hand out the union flyers himself, Lenny was relieved that the flyers had been widely distributed and security had so far not been able to identify the perpetrators. He sent a text message to Gloria, Regis and Moose, suggesting they meet in the employee parking lot after their shifts ended.

A furious Joe West called the entire security department to the office and berated them for letting the union get away with the illegal action. He told his officers they were to confiscate any copies of the flyers they saw and report any worker in possession of one to their supervisor for disciplinary action.

West was not surprised when he was ordered to appear in President Reichart's office at 4 pm sharp, he had been expecting the call. He wasn't worried about the tirade awaiting him, his plan to finally eliminate the pesky shop steward was still on track, despite his men losing track of the major irritant. West was confident Lenny Moss's own predictable actions on Saturday would be his downfall.

In the laundry room Evie picked up one of the union flyers and read it slowly, her reading skills not her strongest asset. She was puzzled that the flyer called for a march to City Hall and a demonstration there. Joe West had been certain the union would try something bold inside James Madison, but the flyer said nothing about that.

Loading up a washing machine, Evie called out to her co-worker, "Say Glory, how come we ain't doin' nothin' here at the hospital? The paper says we're goin' to Center City. That don't make no sense!"

Gloria stopped stacking clean bed sheets on a cart. "Why you askin' me? All I know is what's on the flyer, you were at the union meeting, same as me."

"Yeah, but you're tight with the union. I see you always talking to Lenny Moss. Aren't we gonna do some kinda protest right here at James Madison?"

Gloria had noticed that Evie spoke of the union as a 'we' for the first time. She had never included herself in union affairs before, Evie was always talking about getting out and working in the suburbs at Swanky Lanky. The sudden switch in language raised a suspicion in Gloria's mind.

"At the meeting they talked about calling out the mayor and the governor for not speaking out about the hospitals threatening to take away our benefits. Nobody said anything about marching on Hahnemann or Temple or James Madison."

"Huh. That's all they gonna do?" Evie set the machine and pressed the start switch. "Don't seem too smart to me, it's the hospital taking away our pension and such, not the mayor."

"Well..." Gloria stepped closer to Evie and spoke in a whisper. "I'm not supposed to be telling you this, but I heard from Lenny that the union's gonna sit down in the street in front of City Hall and block traffic. They want to get big time TV coverage on the six o'clock news."

"Is that a fact? That's gonna get a passel of people arrested."

"The union knows that. Thing is, we lose our pensions and our health insurance, we'll have one foot in the grave and the other in a city shelter."

Evie pushed her cart loaded with fresh linen toward the elevator, relieved she had some valuable news for Joe West, and praying it was enough to get her into the dialysis tech program.

Miss Gittens was sipping her cup of tea, not having much of an appetite. Although her stomach no longer cramped, she had little interest in food. What was the point? She remembered her mother and her aunt wasting away, unable to eat and in constant pain. Cancer. What an ugly word.

What an ugly disease.

Mimi came into the room and saw Miss Gittens hadn't touched her scrambled eggs or toast. "Not hungry this morning?" she asked.

Gittens put on a brave smile. "No, not hungry, thank you, Mimi."

"What about some oatmeal? Or maybe some cold cereal and milk?"

"No thank you, dear, I'll just sip my tea and sit awhile."

Stepping out to the hall, Mimi sent a text message to Dr. Green, telling him she was concerned that Miss Gittens was not eating and seemed depressed. Two minutes later she received the doctor's reply: will make rounds right after clinic. Thank you for the update, good job, nurse!

Mimi smiled, knowing that although her patient was facing a tough round of chemo and most likely surgery, she had a wonderful Attending physician on her side. She uttered a silent prayer for a miracle: that the cancer would be responsive to therapy and give the patient some time. A year...two years.

Evie was stacking fresh laundry in the dialysis unit closet when she sensed a presence behind her. A feeling of dread came over her. Turning, she drew in her breath, startled to find Joe West standing a foot behind her.

"You haven't given me my daily report," said West.

"I'm sorry, Mister West, I was going to come see you. It's just we've been so busy down the laundry, I haven't had time to take any kind of a break."

Leading the frightened woman out to the hall, West demanded she give him some news.

"Well, I did talk to my friend Gloria, she's real tight with Lenny Moss."

"What did you find out?"

"Glory said the union was gonna have a sit down in the street outside City Hall. They're gonna block the traffic and raise a great big ruckus, get them on the six o'clock news."

West stared at Evie with his dead shark eyes.

"You're sure they aren't planning anything at James Madison? No demonstration inside the facility."

"No, sir. Glory swore they would all be down Center City, not up here in Mount Airy-Germantown."

Convinced that his snitch was telling him the truth as far as she knew it, West turned and walked away. He exited the ward by the stairwell, not liking to wait for an elevator. Besides, when he used the elevator the workers knew where he was and where he got off. He preferred moving throughout the hospital unseen and unheard.

23

Lenny was wiping down a discharge bed when his cell phone vibrated. Looking at the caller ID, he cursed, seeing it was Detective Williams.

"Moss? Williams here."

"I don't have any new information if that's what you're calling about."

"I called to give you a heads up. The District Attorney is going to issue an arrest warrant for Anna Louisa Mendoza. It sounds like he'll serve the arrest soon. On Monday, maybe. I felt I owed you a call about it."

"Shit. I was afraid of that. Nothing you can do to hold him off, I suppose."

"It's not my decision who to indict, even if I thought your friend acted without intent to harm somebody."

"Christ, that only gives me the weekend to dig up any new evidence!" said Lenny. He thought about the upcoming demonstration on Saturday. Dealing with the fallout would make it all but impossible for him to do much investigating over the weekend.

"You think she did it, don't you?" said Lenny. "You think she killed Landry, by accident or by design."

"Look, I'd be happy to consider an alternative theory, just give me one that makes sense. The rigor mortis tells me she lied about checking on the victim at six. What else is she lying about?"

"She isn't lying, that's the part you don't get." Lenny wished he could convince the detective of Anna's innocence, but so far his investigation was hitting a brick wall. Except...

"There is one thing," said Lenny. "You examined the sharps containers security removed from seven-o-six, and the one from the nurse's medication cart, didn't you?"

Williams laughed. "There's not much gets past you, is there, Moss?"

"I do what I can."

"Yes, I retrieved the containers and their contents."

"You didn't find a used insulin syringe in them, did you?"

"No, I didn't find an insulin syringe. Doesn't prove anything."

"It proves everything! A nurse always drops a syringe into the nearest sharps box, it's drilled into them from day one. Infection control lectures them all the time about needle stick injuries."

"The absence of evidence could simply mean she knew the syringe would incriminate her so she discarded it someplace else. On another floor, even."

"Sure she would, if she was a cold blooded killer. You and I both know she's not. She's a good nurse who goes to church and never gets into trouble."

When the detective started to object, Lenny predicted Anna's fingerprints weren't on the insulin bottle, either. Williams said that proved nothing, Anna would have been wearing latex gloves, but Lenny countered that she wouldn't wear a glove just to pull a bottle of medication out of a medication drawer.

"And one more thing," said Lenny, irritated that the detective was not coming around when it was obvious Anna was an innocent victim. "Did you check the lot number on the bottle of insulin? You might get some idea how it got into the drawer if you knew where it was last used."

Williams admitted he hadn't examined the lethal bottle of insulin that carefully and said he would track it down. He agreed, Anna was an unlikely murder suspect. But in his mind a criminally negligent homicide charge fit the facts; nothing else did.

This time Lenny had no answer to the inevitable conclusion that Anna had caused the death of Mr. Landry. By accident and without intent he was sure, but there was just no other explanation he could come up with. He hung up on the cop, dejected and angry.

Lenny was tempted to give up the investigation, his plate was full and overflowing with the upcoming demonstration. There were the retired seniors, many with serious health problems. Could he ask them to risk arrest, maybe even being pepper sprayed, in a sharp confrontation with hospital security? Joe West would like nothing better than to rough up some of the union members.

And there were the workers with a lot of years on the job — could he ask them to risk everything on a job action the union wasn't authorizing? Lenny returned to his duties troubled by the threats swirling around his brothers and sisters.

With a light tap on the open door, Dr. Green stepped into Miss Gittens' room and pulled a chair up to the bedside. "Good morning, my dear Miss Gittens. How are you feeling today?"

The patient put on a brave smile for her physician, whom she loved dearly. But her sad eyes, close to tears, gave away her true feelings.

"Mimi tells me you haven't been eating of late. You can't fight off those nasty cancer cells if you don't have good nutrition. Don't you think?"

Miss Gittens told him she understood a healthy diet was important in her present state of health, but she didn't believe there was much point eating healthy food when all the spinach and fresh fruit in the world would not turn her cancer into healthy tissue.

"True, true, there's much in what you say, my dear. But I have come with good news! No need to be so sad, your lab tests are very encouraging!"

"Encouraging? How can that be, you said that I have a malignant tumor. I know what that means, it means it is deadly. I know it is the end of me, doctor."

Green took her hand in his and suppressed an urge to kiss her. "Yes, you do have a malignant carcinoma. But — and this is a very big but — the genetic markers in your cancer tell us that is likely to be susceptible to two new therapeutic agents. One is a poison, that will be unpleasant to undergo but I am sure you can bear it, and the other is a new drug that revs up your immune system exactly where you need it to be more active. The medication will help your body fight off the cancer."

Miss Gittens looked into her doctor's eyes. She had seen her mother and aunt die slow, painful deaths from cancer; had been certain she would meet a similar fate. It was all but impossible for her to accept Dr. Green's promises, much as she believed in him.

"Are you really sure the new treatment will help me?"

"'Sure' is a tricky word. We don't talk in certainties when we are dealing with cancer. But the literature and the latest studies are very, very encouraging. I don't want to give you a statistical prediction, the treatments are too new for that. Let's leave it at the fact that your particular strain of cancer looks very much like one that will respond favorably to the treatment. Okay?"

Tears welling in her eyes, Miss Gittens kissed her doctor's hand. He gave hers a little squeeze, smiled, and made his way out.

At the nursing station Dr. Green saw Mimi. When he told her the encouraging news about Gittens, the nurse offered a prayer of thanks. She was so happy for her patient's improved prognosis, she didn't even swear beneath her breath when the dispatcher squawked into her ear that a patient needed 'help, ' the specific nature of the need going unsaid.

<>><><>

Dr. Fahim approached Mr. Manwatty's bed to ask Gary Tuttle how many of the new antibiotics he had administered.

"The third one is almost finished," Gary told him, pointing at the small IV bag hanging from the pole at the bedside.

"Excellent!" Fahim looked at the urine collected in the bag. "He is still making at least thirty cc's an hour, yes?"

"He has a good urine output, Dr. Fahim."

Leaning over the bed, the doctor said, "How are you tolerating the new BIPAP mask, my friend? Not too tight?"

Manwatty gave Fahim a thumbs up gesture.

"Good man. Do not be fearful, the new drugs we are giving you will soon have you feeling much better. Then I can put you back on a regular mask. Okay?"

The young patient nodded his head yes, a wan smile showing beneath the mask with elastic straps that held it tightly against his face so that the ventilator could assist his breathing with a positive pressure flow of oxygen.

Out of the patient's hearing, Gary asked Dr. Fahim when did he think the patient would show signs of improvement. The physician told him he hoped that Manwatty would require less ventilator and intravenous support by the morning, "If the good ID doctor is correct. If we are in fact treating TB."

24

Coming through Seven South to pick up the last of the late lunch trays, Moose found Lenny mopping the floor in a patient room whose toilet had overflowed.

"Yo, Lenny, I hear Joe West is spitting mad about how we got past him with the flyers. He's offering a two week paid vacation to the guard that can nail your ass and get you fired for good."

"Yeah, I heard about it. We have to be careful, Moose, a cornered animal is a dangerous beast." Lenny pointed to the security guard stationed at the junction of Seven south and her sister unit Seven north. "They've been watching me like a hawk. A guard searched my housekeeping closet and my locker."

"Heh, heh. That's why I told you not to carry any flyers out with you. You keep playing it cool, West won't get jack on you, trust me."

Lenny confirmed he would see Moose after work in the parking lot and rolled his mop and bucket on to the next room.

<><><>

Maribel was playing with her schoolmates on the playground when she saw her father standing by the entrance. Maribel stood frozen in place for a moment. She knew the instructions her mother had given her: that she was not to meet with Jimmy or even talk to him except when Anna was present. She wasn't even supposed to visit his Facebook page, though sometimes when she was at her girlfriend's apartment she did take advantage of the computer there, which had no 'parental controls' restricting her web browsing. What she read on his page didn't seem so bad, he just liked to go to parties and have fun, what was wrong with that, everybody wanted to have fun.

Walking over to the entrance, she saw Jimmy had a beautiful white flower with a long green stem in his hand. When she reached him, Jimmy bent down and kissed the top of her head.

"How is my best girl?" he said. "Are you learning lots of cool stuff in your school?"

Maribel shrugged. "I guess so. I don't like the math problems, they make my head hurt."

"They make my head hurt, too." He held the flower out to her. "I brought this for you, do you like it?"

She did like the flower, it was beautiful and it smelled sweet, like her mother's perfume. But she was afraid she would make Anna angry if she accepted a gift from her father.

"Go ahead, take it," he said. When Maribel still hesitated, Jimmy assured her she would not get in trouble. "Pack it in your lunch box. If Anna asks where you found it, say your teacher gave it to you."

"But papi, that would be telling a lie, wouldn't it?"

"No, no, it wouldn't be a lie because you are keeping a secret. It is just for you and me to know and no one else. When two people are keeping a secret, they cannot tell anyone else about it, so they have to make up a story. But it is not really a lie, it is a secret."

When Maribel still hesitated, he added, "Hey, cariño, I

am your one and only original father, remember? It will be okey-dokey. I swear!"

Maribel took the flower just as the teacher blew her whistle calling the children back to class. Maribel put the flower in her lunch box so she would not have to make up a story for her teacher about who gave it to her. Not that she had been a bad girl to accept a gift from Jimmy. After all, he was her one and only original father.

After putting away his mop and bucket for the day, Lenny walked over to room 706 one more time. He hated to give up on Anna and accept that she had lied to him. Over the years he had heard many a worker telling false stories when they were in trouble with the supervisor. A few of them were good liars, but most were bad at it, making it easier for the boss to catch them in a lie and sustain any disciplinary action that might otherwise have been reversed in a grievance.

Anna had seemed so honest and decent when he interviewed her. And Mimi was a good judge of character, Lenny had a lot of respect for her opinion. With the arrest warrant coming on Monday, Lenny was determined to try and find some logical explanation for how Landry died. And for who killed him.

He saw Mimi wheeling her medication cart into the med room. Catching the door before it closed behind the nurse, he slipped into the room.

"Hey," he said in a low whisper.

Surprised, Mimi opened her mouth to speak, but held her voice when she saw Lenny holding a finger to his lips.

"Battery?" Lenny whispered, pointing at the GPS unit hanging from the nurse's neck. Mimi popped out the battery and set it down on her cart.

"What's up?" she asked.

Lenny explained that he was still unable to come up with an alternative explanation for Landry's death, but he couldn't bring himself to give up on Anna. "Tell me one more time exactly what happened the morning you found him."

Mimi closed her eyes, visualizing the scene. She told him about seeing Mr. Landry lying on his back with his eyes and his mouth open. "It was an unnatural posture, know what I mean? Most patients sleep on their side," she said, opening her eyes. "So I checked to see if he was breathing, and when I found he wasn't I checked his pulse. It was absent."

Lenny pictured the scene, having cleaned up the debris surrounding a corpse after more than a few codes.

"You didn't see any sign of the insulin syringe. It wasn't lying around."

"No, I didn't see any syringe of any kind."

"I'm bothered the police got hold of the two sharps container we talked about, they didn't find an insulin syringe. Security had the containers first, they could have emptied them and removed any incriminating evidence. But I can't see West doing that, he wouldn't have anything to do with a wrongful death, it would hurt the hospital's reputation."

"Unless they found a syringe and it had somebody else's prints on it," said Mimi.

"Yeah, you're right, that West is capable of anything."

Lenny stared at the disabled GPS unit, wishing the dead patient had been on a cardiac monitor. But he knew wishing for the impossible was a big time waste of his time and energy.

"Okay, what happened next?"

"Oh, man, then I cursed and let out a yell. I was afraid the patient in B bed would hear me cursing, I was so excited about finding Mister Landry dead, but lucky for me, B bed was empty."

"That's right, there wasn't another patient who might have seen what really happened. Damn."

As he turned to go, Mimi grabbed Lenny's arm. "Are they really going to arrest Anna and charge her?"

"Yeah, afraid so. It sounds like the District Attorney is probably looking at involuntary manslaughter, I don't think they see her as intending to kill anybody, but still..."

"It's total bad news for Anna. And for her daughter. Anna told me once Jimmy could sweet talk anybody into buying what he was selling, but it was all for show. Inside, it's all about what's good for him."

"Not uncommon in a salesman, I suppose," said Lenny.

Lenny headed toward the housekeeping locker room, discouraged about the case and with no idea how he could solve it. He tried to prepare himself for the worst — that Anna would be arrested, maybe on Monday, and there was nothing he could do to prevent it.

25

After punching out at the time clock, Lenny met Moose, Regis and Gloria in the employee parking lot. They sat in Lenny's car, ignoring the security guard watching them from the guard station, a cell phone camera pointed at them.

"We're all set for the demonstration tomorrow," said Moose. "Everybody says they're coming."

Gloria said, "Everyone in the laundry will be there, except for Evie, she's a snitch, I'm sure of it." She told them about her co-worker's sudden expression of union loyalty and the false story about locking traffic in Center City outside City Hall she had given the snitch.

"Smart move," said Lenny. "West probably won't buy it, he's no fool, but still, it may throw him off a little."

"How're we getting from the union hall to the hospital?" said Regis.

"The union will give out bus passes. Our people will ride up Germantown Ave to James Madison, the others will go to Temple or Hahnemann." Lenny told them how security had searched him, his housekeeping closet and his locker.

"Man, I wish I could've seen West's face when they told him they lost track of you with all the guys wearing hoodies," said Regis. "I bet he was one pissed off son of a bitch."

"It was a good move," said Lenny. "I'm glad Moose talked me into not carrying any flyers. I didn't like it, but it was the right thing to do." He reminded them that even though they had strong support from the rank and file, they still needed to call co-workers that evening and be sure they were coming to the demonstration the next morning.

Agreeing to meet at the union headquarters the next day at 12 pm to set out the banner and signs, Regis and Gloria left the car, leaving Moose alone with his friend.

"How far we gonna push it tomorrow?" said Moose.

Lenny put the key in the ignition and turned it. The starter labored to turn over the engine, but the spark didn't fire it up.

"Need new plugs? he asked.

"More like a new car. Patience is bugging me to get something newer. She wants a convertible."

"Gotta get the woman what she wants, you don't need her breaking down at night down in Germantown. Or North Philly."

Lenny tried the starter again. This time the engine fired up, though it idled rough.

"What do you think we should do tomorrow?" Lenny asked.

"I think we should march to the president's office, like we did once before, tell him he got to keep our benefits. This ain't no game, it's a matter of life or death."

"Reichart probably won't be in his office on a Saturday."

"Makes no difference, he'll hear about it from whatever bozo they got in charge. He'll get the message."

"The retirees are fired up. You saw them at the union hall, they're mad as hell."

"Hornets in a swarm got nothin' on them," said Moose. "If the seniors turn out for the demonstration and march down the executive suite, they'll scare the crap outta the bosses."

"They scare the hell out of me," said Lenny. He bid Moose good-night and drove to the parking lot exit. Seeing that the guard was still recording his movements on his cell phone, Lenny had a sudden moment of inspiration. He stopped the car, took out his own cell, and stepped out of the car. He opened the camera app, set it to video mode, and pointed it at the guard.

Walking slowly toward the guard in the little security station, Lenny said out loud, "You are seeing one of James Madison's finest security guards, who has been recording my movements since I clocked in to work this morning."

Flummoxed, the guard hesitated, then lowered his phone and put it in his pocket.

"From now on I will be snapping photos and short video clips of the James Madison security apparatus as they follow me around the hospital and post them online. Maybe they will find a better way to use their time, like to protect the patients and staff from trespassers with criminal intentions."

He got back in his car and drove out onto Germantown Ave. As the tires thumped and rattled on the old cobblestone sections of the street, holdovers from the days of trolley car service, Lenny allowed himself a moment of satisfaction. Not that the fight was over, but at least he was hitting back for a change.

President Reichart had Joe West standing in front of him in his office, and the CEO was not happy. "You said you have a plan to arrest Lenny Moss and terminate him. Is that plan going to come to fruition?"

West assured his boss his plan was a good one. The security chief well understood his job depended on getting rid of the pesky shop steward. He had to trap Moss in a way that brought criminal charges against the man. That was the only way to be sure the union would lose any grievance, even if it went to a state mediator. West knew that breaking Lenny was the key to breaking the union at James Madison.

"Do you know yet what his plans are for their demonstration?" said Reichart. "I presume they will be coming to James Madison."

"My sources don't have an accurate picture of their plans yet, but —"

"No accurate picture? What do you think I pay you for, reading horoscopes?"

West stood stone still. He was not in the habit of failing. In this respect, he and Reichart were much alike.

"I have another resource I can tap."

"Get it done. I'm anticipating sympathetic press coverage, their friends in the media are always willing to paint the unions in a positive light. I want you to be sure that Moss and his cronies step over the line. They need to look like troublemakers. Terrorists. You understand?"

"Yes sir, I understand."

Reichart turned his attention to his computer, signaling he was done with West, who hurried out of the office. West summoned his most loyal and brutal security guard. Whenever West needed somebody roughed up and intimidated, Horace was his man.

At home that evening, Lenny made several calls to co-workers about tomorrow's demonstration. He said to a young lab tech who was more scared about losing his job to cutbacks than losing his pension benefits, "Do you know how much it will cost you to pay for your health care benefits if the whole fee comes out of your pocket?"

The tech said he was healthy, he probably wouldn't need the benefits for a long time.

"Well, you play a lot of sports, don't think you can visit the ER without a monster bill," said Lenny. "The hospital will attach your pay and ruin your credit rating if you don't cover the bill."

He had just hung up on the young tech when his phone rang. He saw on the caller ID the name of his former housekeeping partner, Betty, who was now retired.

"Yo, Lenny! What you been up to? You kickin' the boss's butt, like always?"

"Hi, Betty, how're you doing?"

"I'm doin' as good as The Lord gives me strength to carry on. How's that sweet wife o' yours? Tell me Patience ain't kicked your sorry ass out the house n' changed the locks?"

"No, Patience is still putting up with me. I don't know why, but as long as she's keeping me, I'm not going anywhere."

"You two are blessed with a nice family. I'm happy for you. Now give me the straight talk, we gonna march into the president's office an' give him hell? 'Cause I'm ready to kick some butt, you best believe it!"

Lenny told her the official union plan was to go to City Hall for a rally, but if some members were to break away 'spontaneously' and go to the hospital, he guessed he would go with them.

"You can count me in! I'll be bringing Big Mary, she can't yell, but she can still make a racket with her good hand. We got a whole lot of retirees coming, you can count on us!"

Lenny thanked his old housekeeping partner and said good-night, encouraged that retirees like her were coming to the demonstration. He answered a dozen more calms, including one from the union VP, who assured Lenny the union would back him 100% should he or any other members require legal assistance.

Lenny was encouraged so many workers, active and retired, were supporting the demonstration. Several promised to bring their family members, which always made for good photos in the paper. He didn't know how far they would take it when the members entered the hospital on their day off, which was every day as far as the retirees were concerned. Well, he and Moose would just have to gauge the sentiment of the demonstrators and make a judgement call.

When Malcolm overheard Lenny talking to some of the union members on the phone, he understood Saturday would be a big day for the union and for his mom and dad.

"Lenny?" the boy asked when Lenny finally turned off his cell phone and poured himself a drink.

"Can I come to the demonstration tomorrow?" Lenny hesitated. "I ain't got school, it's Saturday."

"I know what day it is, and don't let your mother hear you saying 'I ain't got school', she'll throw a fit."

"Yeah, okay, I'll watch it. You gonna let me go?"

Lenny pulled the boy closer. A step-father, he loved Malcolm as deeply as any father could, biological or not.

"Actually, this is the one time you and Takia can join me and your mom, the union is asking everybody to bring their family with them to the event." Seeing the look of joy coming over Malcolm's face, Lenny added, "But, if I go into the hospital at some point, you and your mother and sister will stay outside on the sidewalk. You understand?"

"I wanna stay with you, Lenny! I wanna kick the boss's

ass like you do!"

Lenny kissed the boy on the top of his head and released him. "Time enough for the rough stuff when you're eighteen. Until then, you stay on the sidewalk and keep out of trouble."

"O-kay," said Malcolm, disappointed he couldn't join Lenny on the march into the hospital. But still he found satisfaction in finally joining his parents in a real life action with the union.

He was going to be as brave and tough as the action figures he played with.

And as bold as Lenny Moss.

26

On Saturday morning, Lenny woke up at five am, as he did every morning, even on his day off. When he and Patience went on vacation he always needed a week to get his body used to sleeping late. By then it was time to go back to work.

Slipping silently out of bed so as not to wake his wife, he put on a robe and old leather slippers and went downstairs to make coffee. Once the kettle was on the flame, he turned on his cell phone and checked his messages. There were ten. Not a surprise, given today was the day of the big demonstration.

While the coffee was brewing he answered his text messages, assuring the retirees they would have a ride from the union hall to the demonstration. He confirmed with Moose when to meet at the hall. And he confirmed with the union VP that "all the plans were in place," meaning the clandestine plan to march on the hospital in an "unsanctioned" action.

Patience joined him at the kitchen table. "You really think it'll be safe bringing Malcolm to the demonstration? He's awfully young."

"My parents took me to peace vigils when I was younger than Malcolm. It'll be a good experience for him. Besides, he's been bugging me to go to a union activity for a long time."

Lenny promised his wife that when and if a group broke away from the public demonstration and went into the hospital, he would tell Malcolm he had to stay on the sidewalk with Patience. He didn't want the child with him if some of West's goons decided to play rough.

He remembered a strike from years ago. Lenny had been a strike captain on the night shift when a trio of goons stepped out of a van and approached him carrying baseball bats. They were not looking for a ball to hit.

During the planning stages leading up to that strike, Moose had said to Lenny, "The boss has got some bad ass brawlers who will try to beat up on people. We got to have our own bad ass brawlers, too."

They agreed to always have at least four or five of the toughest union members on hand at the picket line, day or night. If there were only a handful of picketers at night, half of them would have to be fighters.

When the three goons approached Lenny and the women from laundry and housekeeping who were with him, he was relieved to have four comrades standing with him. Imo was a black belt martial arts expert, Raj was a street fighter who could beat a man twice his size, and the other two were long time bar fighters with fists like pistons in a ship's engine.

The union men didn't wait for the goons to attack. Instead, they leaped on the three troublemakers, with the women throwing punches along with the men. The goons were lucky to escape with their lives, and the fight became a legend repeated over and over at union meetings and parties. Especially at parties.

"Malcolm will be fine," Lenny reiterated. "He will be well protected."

<> <> <>

Leading his Infectious Disease team into the ICU, Dr. Auginello greeted Fahim, who met him at the nursing station.

"Good morning, Michael," said the critical care Attending. "No tie this morning, I see."

"Morning, Samir. It's Saturday. I give myself permission to dress casual on the weekend."

"Why don't you wear scrubs like me? They are very comfortable."

"Perhaps one day I will. But tell me about Manwatty, I saw that his lactate level has dropped and his blood gas is improved."

"His fever broke last night, he has defervesced beautifully. This morning I am going to take him off the external bipap and switch him to a conventional oxygen mask."

"His blood gas has improved that much?"

"See for yourself, my friend." Fahim opened the lab report on the computer and scrolled down to the patient's blood gas. The latest pH and arterial oxygen values were significantly improved. "His lactate is also trending down," Fahim said, scrolling to another report.

Auginello asked his resident to call up the patient's latest serum drug levels on the computer, since the patient had produced sub-therapeutic values when he had been on oral medications. The levels for the intravenous antibiotic drugs were all in the therapeutic range.

"No results on the TB culture yet?" he asked.

The resident confirmed, the culture was not back yet.

"Your house staff must be learning great patience," said Fahim. "Tuberculosis is a very slow growing bacteria."

"It's a hard lesson to learn. Harder for the patient, though, he has to wait to learn if I came up with the correct diagnosis, or sent him to an early grave."

"It is TB!" said Fahim. "Of this I have no doubt. No doubt whatsoever!"

Going to the bedside, Auginello listened to the patient's breath sounds, noted the heart rate and rhythm, and checked Manwatty's ankles for signs of edema. While he conducted his examination, the respiratory therapist, a slender redhead wearing clogs and pink scrubs that complimented her red hair, removed the positive pressure mask, switched off the ventilator, and placed an ordinary oxygen mask over Manwatty's face.

"That's much better, isn't it?" said Auginello.

Manwatty nodded his head. "It is very much better, thank you, doctor."

"Feel like eating something?"

"I would dearly love a cup of tea. With milk, if that is allowed." Turning to the nurse, he added, "And perhaps I could have a little sugar?"

"You can have all the sugar you want," said Gary Tuttle. As the nurse went to the kitchen to make the tea, Auginello suggested he bring some eggs and toast. "If you can take in a little nourishment, it will help your body fight off the infection. Think you can get down some food?"

"I will try my best, doctor."

The ID Attending patted the patient on the shoulder. At the nursing station he updated his progress notes, noting the marked improvement in temperature, blood pressure and heart rate. He signed the note, closed the chart and signaled for his resident and Fellow to follow, they had many more patients to see before their day was through. And he was going to damned well try and stay at the hospital until the TB culture came back. If it turned out to be negative, it would encourage Slocum and Reichart to further erode the authority of the physicians. That was not a clinical setting in which he wanted to practice medicine.

<><><>

Anna called the bus company to listen to the recorded message announcing when the bus would arrive from Florida. Even though her mother had told her the time, Anna wanted to be sure and get there in plenty of time in case the bus arrived early.

Maribel asked if they should pack a sandwich for grandma. "She might be hungry after her trip, it is a long way to Philadelphia, isn't it?"

"That is a good idea, we will take her something to eat. I will buy some tamales from Cocina's, they make them fresh on Saturday."

"What about a bottle of chocolate milk? She will be thirsty, too!"

Anna smiled and gently ran her hand over the top of Maribel's head. "Another good idea! And if grandma is not so very thirsty, I think maybe you can help her finish the chocolate milk. And the tamales."

Maribel agreed, she would help finish any food that grandma did not want. "It is a sin to waste food, is it not, mama?"

"Si, mi hija pequeña, it is a sin."

27

At the union hall, President Echols greeted the members and their families with a rousing speech that recalled the union's early days, the long first strike that lasted through the Christmas and New Year's holidays, and the current administrations that were skimming off profits while trying to cut benefits and eliminate their pensions.

"They want to take away our prescription benefits while they receive million dollar salaries and golden parachutes when they leave!" he cried. "They want you to live on charity or in a shelter when they cut off your pension checks! They look down on you as unworthy and disposable. They even want to cut the heart out of the doctors' practice and let a computer practice medicine!"

Cheers and catcalls echoed as the president went on. "You see the GPS units the nurses are forced to wear. The bosses want to put them on everybody! They want to track your body every second like you were a package in a UPS delivery truck. Well we aren't packages and we aren't robots, we are human beings, and we demand the respect and dignity that every human being on God's earth deserves!"

The crowd stood and cheered. They hooted and hollered. The retirees knocked the floor with their canes and cried glory hallelujah.

When the members finally quieted down and took their seats, Echols told them the union's plan for the day. They would all be given tokens to take buses down Broad Street to City Hall. There the union would hold a rally, where members of the City Council and several clergy members would speak in support of their campaign to save their union benefits and pension.

"Now, brothers and sister, I will see that you all receive bus tokens for you and for your family members. But the union is not like the bosses at the hospital. We can't make you get on the bus and ride down town, and we won't demand that you use the tokens for that purpose." With a sly smile on his face, Echols added, "If some of you end up going in a different direction on the bus, well, brothers and sisters, nobody is going to criticize you for that. You go where your heart and your conscience send you, and God bless everyone who follows their heart."

The president looked at Lenny and Moose, who understood, that was their cue. The two men got up, signaled to the coworkers they could see in the crowd, and began walking out of the hall. They led the James Madison workers across the street to the side that was heading away from Center City, up toward Mt. Airy and the hospital. Several members followed the union leadership to the downtown bus, but more than half followed Lenny and Moose.

As the first bus came to a stop, Moose suggested they let the seniors go first. It was a slow progression, a few of the retirees employed walkers to assist them, and two had oxygen tanks. When the bus was finally filled and pulling away, Lenny saw Big Mary in her wheelchair being pushed by Betty, his former housekeeping partner. Mary had a sign tied to the back of her wheelchair that read, SAVE OUR BENEFITS! Lenny complimented her on the sign. "We'll get you two on the next bus," he said. Looking at the swelling group around the stop, he realized they would need two or three more buses to get everybody up to the hospital.

"Say Lenny," said Stella, a retiree sporting a thick, knobby cane. "Has the union got a porta-poddy outside the hospital? Some of us got to go more times than others."

"No, sorry, but you can use the bathrooms inside the main lobby, it shouldn't be a problem."

Reassured, she leaned on her cane and gazed down Germantown Ave, looking for the next bus.

Gloria was standing in line for the bus to go to the hospital when she felt a tap on her shoulder. Turning, she was surprised to see Evie.

"Ain't you goin' the wrong way? City Hall is that-away?" Evie said.

"We're going up to the hospital, give 'em a piece of our mind."

"What you gonna do there? I'd come along, but I don't want to get in no trouble."

"We're gonna demonstrate in front of the hospital. Then a delegation is going to have a little talk with the benefits office over at Human Resources. We're gonna tell them what would happen if they took our benefits away. They have to understand, this is a matter of life and death."

"I thought you were gonna stop traffic down City Hall."

"No, we gave up that idea. At City Hall it'll just be a picket line."

"Oh. Well, I'll feel safer down town, I don't wanna lose my job for demonstrating at the hospital."

Evie crossed the street and joined a small groups of workers going to Center City. As soon as she was out of Gloria's sight, she took out her cell phone and called the hospital security office. "Lemme talk to Mister West! It's important!" After a long wait, she heard the West's hard voice, and was afraid.

<><><>

Dr. Auginello and his team were rounding on their last patient, an elderly man on isolation for scabies. The physician remarked that the nurses all started to itch as soon as they heard their patient was infested with the mites. "It's not that easy to contract," he assured them. "It requires close physical contact, skin to skin, but the staff always worry they will pick it up and take it home with them to their family."

"I notified the Department of Health," said the intern. "They are going to investigate the nursing home where the patient lives."

"Good. The DOH will order treatment for the other clients." He recommended to the Hospitalist team responsible for the patient's care a topical treatment along with an oral medication that would circulate in the blood and suppress the mites that sucked on the host's blood. Looking forward to a a quiet Saturday afternoon with his wife, he said, "If there are no more consults to follow..."

The ID Fellow signaled to him. "Doctor Auginello, the TB culture is back on Mister Manwatty."

Auginello tucked his collection of three-by-five cards with his current case load into his lab coat pocket, stepped over to the portable computer the Fellow had been using, and looked at the screen. A smiled curled his lips.

Positive.

The urine and blood cultures had finally shown a positive growth, which meant there was evidence of bacteria in the culture medium. The follow up gene probe came back positive for tuberculosis. Auginello's diagnosis was confirmed, Teepee had been wrong. His gamble on administering anti-TB drugs without clear clinical signs of tuberculosis had paid off. This time there would be no diagnosis of disseminated TB made post mortem in the autopsy suite.

"Congratulations, Doctor Auginello," the Fellow said.

"Thank you, Ramon. We dodged a bullet on this one."

The satisfied physician instructed his Fellow on what clinical issues to follow while on call Saturday night and all day Sunday. "Call me if you run into any problems," he said, heading off the ward.

The Fellow promised to stop back in the ICU to share the victory with Dr. Fahim and the nursing staff. "And of course, I will tell Mister Manwatty for you," he added.

Auginello strode toward the elevators, whistling an old standard from the American song book. He was looking forward to sitting out on his backyard deck, smoking a good celebratory cigar and enjoying two fingers of excellent bourbon.

He might even throw a few steaks on the outdoor grill.

28

A young security guard stationed in the main lobby was reading an email message from his girlfriend on his cell phone when he heard voices coming from outside the front door. Looking up, he saw a posse of seniors walking up the broad marble steps. Startled, the guard hurried to the front door and peered out through the glass, astounded by what he saw.

Betty pushed Big Mary in her wheelchair up the long ramp, with the partially paralyzed Mary using her good arm to help turn one of the big wheels. Moose Maddox had his strong arm around a retired chef who was struggling up the steps with his walker. Lenny carried a green, wheeled oxygen tank up the steps for a former housekeeper, who huffed and puffed as she lifted her swollen legs up the steps. When they had all gotten off the buses and assembled outside the hospital they discussed who would go into the hospital and who would stay outside. All of the retirees and half the currently employed workers volunteered to go in, while the remaining members and the family members picketed outside on the sidewalk.

"Okay, everyone!" Lenny called out as the last stragglers came up the broad steps and passed through the entrance, "let's gather inside the lobby!"

Holding one of the doors open, Lenny ushered in the last of the protesting seniors. He counted sixty-four by the time the last one had shuffled through the door using a walker.

The lobby was packed wall to wall. To the right a corridor led to the elevators, outpatient suites and the cafeteria; on the left, the hallway led to the administrative wing, including Patient Relations, Security and the President's office.

Stella, red hat askew over wild silver hair, lifted a cane and pointed to the left. "That's where that bastard Reichart has his office! C'mon!" Three more women locked their arms together and followed behind her.

The guard rushed to the middle of the corridor and held his arms out wide to block them. "Hold on there, ladies, you can't enter the administrative offices without an appointment. And you for sure can't bring a mob of people with you."

"This ain't no mob!" cried Luz, a thickly built Puerto Rican who had worked as a nurse's aide. "We're retired workers! We all used to work here, an' we got a right to talk to the boss that's tryin' to put us in our grave!"

"Nobody's going past me," said the guard. "No body."

Stella lifted her cane high above her head and stepped closer to the young guard. Nose to nose, she said, "Teddy Towson, I know your mother! We go to the same church! You want me to tell her what kinda no good, sell out rapscallion her son has turned into? *Huh?*"

"I'm sorry, Miss Stella," said the guard. "I'm just doing my job."

"Job be damned!" said Stella. "We did our job, year after year, day time, night time, weekday, week end. We cleaned and carried and cooked and served, and now that son of a bitch Robert Reichart is talking about taking away our benefits!"

"But, but, they wouldn't really do that, ma'am. Would they?"

"O' course they would," said Tillie, standing beside her

friend. "Ever since Croesus bought out James Madison, all they think about is profit, profit, profit. They don't care if we live or die!"

"An' we'll be dead if we lose our health benefits!" said Luz. "Not to mention we'll be out in the street if we lose our pension, too!"

The guard pulled his walkie-talkie from his belt and called in to the central station alerting them about the large number of retirees massing in the lobby. As he held the device up to his ear trying to hear his instructions above the clamor from the crowd, several seniors surged past the guard. Like a dam bursting, the gang of curmudgeons surged past, overwhelming the young guard. They filled the corridor as they flowed down the hall past the Patient Relations and the Benefits Office.

Reaching a bronze plaque beside an ornate oak door that read "OFFICE OF THE PRESIDENT," they stopped. Stella hesitated, not sure if they should all go in or send a delegation.

"Lenny!" she called out. "What we gonna say if he's there and we see him?"

Lenny squeezed his way through the crowd. "You've been doing great so far, Stella. I couldn't say it any better than you."

"Well stick beside me, brother, I ain't goin' down for this all by my lonesome."

She pushed the door open and marched in with Lenny, Tillie and Luz right behind her. They found the president's secretary seated beside a large desk. She wore a vivid blue business suit, high heels and a perplexed look on her face.

"What...what's going on?" she said, rising from her chair.

"We wanna see the President, and we don't wanna hear no bull shit!" said Stella.

"Uh, I'm sorry, President Reichart is not in the facility today, this is a Saturday."

"Where's he at?" said Stella.

"Uh, I believe he's at a meeting. But not here at the hospital."

"Well call him up and tell him to get his butt up here to the hospital, we need to talk to him," said Luz.

As a few more retirees squeezed into the outer office, followed by a handful of current workers, Moose edged over to the door leading to the president's inner sanctum and tried the handle, but it was locked. Lenny leaned over and told him the door was always locked, the secretary had to buzz you in to get through.

The secretary picked up the phone, but she didn't call her boss on his cell phone or page him. Instead, she called the security office and spoke to the dispatcher. She told him there was a group of angry seniors demanding to see President Reichart.

"We're already aware of the disturbance, we're sending more men to handle it. Is Mister Reichart anywhere in the hospital?" asked the guard.

"No, he's meeting with the architects in Center City. What should I do? Should I call him?"

"Stay put and don't antagonize them," said the guard. "We will notify the President."

The secretary hung up, thinking there wasn't anything she could do that would make the seniors any angrier than they already were.

Robert Reichart was looking over the architectural

plans for the new addition to the hospital, which included an exclusive executive ward with special amenities for elite customers.

"As you can see," said the lead architect, "we have designed the new ward for high income patients who expect the very best, not only in medical care, but in comfort and service. We will offer them concierge service, adjoining guest quarters, a Jacuzzi and a luxury bathroom, and a two-to-one patient-nurse ratio."

"Meals will be cooked individually for each patient," said the director of the kitchen. "And for their guests, of course."

Asked by the chair of the Department of Medicine if the plan wouldn't be providing unequal levels of care, Reichart assured him that the medical care would be the same, only the amenities would be plusher. There would be a dedicated satellite pharmacy with a pharmacist on duty twenty-four seven.

"The clients will even have their own exclusive elevator to use," the architect added. "With an elevator operator who can act as concierge."

The new wing would be a gleaming copper and silver edifice; a monument to Reichart's leadership, having raised the necessary funds and cleared all the pesky environmental regulations. The bonus he expected to receive for downsizing the staff was a satisfying reward in itself, but the new building would be his triumph.

His cell phone chimed a military bugle sound.

Seeing the caller ID was James Madison security, Reichart turned his back on the group and pressed Answer.

"Problem?" Reichart asked.

The security guard said, "Apparently there's a large crowd of senior citizens gathered outside your office!"

"What the hell do they want, a free lunch?"

"I'm told they're hospital retirees, they're complaining about losing their benefits."

Reichart was not surprised at the demonstration in the administrative wing of the hospital, he had suspected Lenny Moss and his minions would try something like that. It was a pointless gesture, the only administrators on duty Saturday morning were the VP for Hospital Affairs and the Chief of Housekeeping.

"What are they doing? Are they occupying the office?"

"No, sir, I don't think so, they're just waiting around for you to come talk to them."

"Tell West to get rid of them. I want every intruder out of the building, voluntarily or in handcuffs, I don't give a damn which, just get them out. I will see West in my office when I've concluded this meeting and returned to the facility. And tell him if that pest Lenny Moss is there I want the man removed. In leg irons."

29

The demonstrators filling the President's outer office and spilling into the hall began a chant. "One, two, three, four, our pension's what we're fighting for!" The lone security guard who had been overwhelmed was soon joined by a half dozen more guards. They sealed off the hallway, blocking the exits and, more importantly, the bathrooms. It was a smart tactic, Lenny wished he'd thought about guarding the toilets.

As the chants continued, a senior security officer sporting a pistol and a bunch of plastic hand cuffs stepped up to the line of demonstrators. "Nobody from the administration is going to meet with a mob. If your union had a complaint, they should have requested a meeting with Human Resources."

"We asked for a meeting a dozen times," said Lenny. "All we got was stone-walling and a lot of BS."

"That's not in my department," said the officer. "My job is to protect the staff and the property in this facility. I have orders for all of you to vacate the premises or you will be charged with criminal trespassing and be taken to jail."

Stella said to Lenny, "I don't mind goin' to the Round House so long as they have a working toilet! I got to take care of business!"

Lenny smiled. In a huddle out of the security guard's hearing he told her he didn't think they should take it so far that everyone was arrested.

"Why don't we take our demonstration through the hospital to the cafeteria?" said Moose. "It's lunch time, we can reach a lot of workers that way."

With the others in agreement, Lenny told the security officer they were leaving. He, Stella and Gloria led the group down the hall toward the lobby, but when they reached the main entrance they continued down the other wing instead of exiting.

"Wait a minute!" cried the guard who had first met them. "Where the hell are you going?"

"Bath room!" said Stella. "Some of us can't wait till the bus gets us home!"

They marched down the hall, with Big Mary in her wheelchair lifting her paralyzed arm in the air with her good hand, a crooked grin on her face, her permanently clenched fist proudly defiant.

Before reaching the cafeteria a few demonstrators rushed into the bathrooms, the ones using canes or walkers being ushered in first, while the rest of them marched on. Once inside the cafeteria, they set up a picket line and marched up and down the center of the room, chanting "Unions yes, bosses, no, Croesus Medical's got to go!"

The startled visitors looked up from their lunch trays, wondering what the commotion was about. Several of the demonstrators handed out flyers that described the threats against their benefits and pensions. The visitors, reading the flyer, expressed their support for the demonstrators, with a few even joining them on the picket line.

The workers on the job taking their lunch break took out cell phones and snapped photos and videos of the demonstrators, which they texted to their co-workers on the wards and in the many departments they represented. Within minutes the whole hospital knew about the demonstration.

Soon, workers throughout the hospital began telling

their supervisors they were going on their lunch break. Employees began streaming into the cafeteria, the different colors of their respective department uniforms forming a rainbow of colors as they joined the demonstrators and marched up and down the cafeteria, chanting and laughing.

Joe West appeared at the end of the room beside the checkout counter. Calling for quiet, West told the demonstrators they were creating a public nuisance and interfering with the operation of the hospital. If they did not leave immediately he would call in the Philadelphia police and have them all arrested for criminal trespass.

"All righty, then," said Gloria. "We'll be quiet, but we're not leaving until we're good and ready to go!"

"That's right," said Lenny. "The cafeteria is open to the public. You can't charge us with trespass in a public cafeteria."

West strode up to Lenny, a menacing look on his face. Moose quickly stepped up beside his friend.

"I'm only saying this once, Moss. This is an illegal assembly. It violates your own union contract. You will take your people out of the building in an orderly fashion, or my officers will begin making arrests."

Before Lenny could argue that their action was not a union sanctioned action, Stella cried out, "We ain't goin! We're getting lunch! C'mon, everybody, get on line for coffee or something, we're staying, they can't arrest us for eating lunch in a god damn cafeteria!"

West turned on his heels and strode out of the cafeteria. Out in the hall his sergeant asked what were they going to do?

"Wait until most of them are through the line with their purchase, then you and Teddy gather up four more officers and arrest Moss and Maddox, they're the leaders. And take that loud mouthed one, the one in the black jacket and red hat. Once we turn them over to the authorities, the others will fold and we'll be rid of them."

"Understood," said the guard. "But what if the others refuse to leave?"

"Then the jail is going to be overrun with seniors."

West strode off to speak to his contact in the police department, telling his officers to make ready for the arrests.

30

Dressed in full riot gear, with plastic face shields and carrying thick truncheons, a troop of Philadelphia police marched through the hospital corridor and entered the cafeteria. Their lieutenant conferred with Joe West while his officers fanned out across the big room, covering the entrance and the exit and blocking anyone from leaving.

"Those are the trespassers?" the lieutenant said, pointing at the people standing in the middle of the room.

"That's pretty much most of them," said West. "A bunch of the seniors have taken a seat, they're trying to blend in with the visitors, but we can identify most of them for you. We've been taking videos, we have all of them on tape."

"There are reporters outside with cameras and TV broadcast trucks," the lieutenant told West. "Apparently some of the hospital employees sent videos to the local news stations. It's not going to look good dragging out a lot of senior citizens. I see a few of them are toting oxygen tanks, for Christ sake."

West gazed at the scene with icy eyes. "You don't have to arrest all of them, just the ringleaders. I'll point them out to you, four or five in cuffs will break their spirit, they'll take off as soon as they see what will happen if they don't comply."

The police lieutenant called over two of his officers and told them the plan. As they passed the word on to the others, the lieutenant stepped up to the front of the line of demonstrators.

"All right, people, listen up! I'm Lieutenant Jeffrey Porter of the Philadelphia Police Department! Mister West has informed me you are none of you employed at this hospital or scheduled to work here today!"

"We got as much right to be here as anybody!" called Stella.

"You do not have a right to disrupt the functioning of the institution. If you do not disperse immediately you will be arrested for criminal trespass, disturbing the peace, and creating a public nuisance!"

"We're not disrupting anything!" said Gloria, stepping up to the officer and standing nose to nose to him. "Everybody's eating and drinking. Nobody's stopping nobody from getting fed. We all ordered food ourselves. We got a right to eat here, the cafeteria's open to the public! Always has been!"

Turning away from Gloria, the police lieutenant stepped back out into the hall to confer with West. The officer pointed out that the cafeteria was open to the public. Visitors, job applicants, salespeople all came there to eat or drink, not just employees on their lunch break.

"But they are disturbing the peace," said West. "They are creating a nuisance. Employees from all over the facility have come down to see what's going on. Look at them, they're taking videos. I have no doubt some of the pictures are already showing up online."

The lieutenant remained skeptical. After further discussion, he suggested to West that they close the cafeteria. "As long as it's closed, they will all have to obey an order to disperse or face a criminal trespass charge."

Irritated that the police officer wanted an excuse to make the arrests, West snapped an order to his sergeant, who informed the manager of the cafeteria that they were closing the department. "For how long?" said the manager, a young red headed woman. "There are still employees coming down for lunch."

"You'll be able to open back up once we've cleared the room of demonstrators. For now, the cafeteria is closed."

The young manger closed the entrance to the serving line and informed the cashiers they would be sent on break as soon the last customers paid for their meals. Asked by a sever if she should pack the food up and take it back to the kitchen, the young woman said her guess was as good as anybody else's, the whole business was nuts.

When the security guard announced the cafeteria was now closed and all occupants must leave, workers who were taking their lunch break refused. "I got a right to eat my lunch! You can't take my break time away from me!" Others yelled their agreement. They held up their plates of food and drinks to show the security guards and police they were eating lunch, as did the retirees.

"All right, you all have fifteen more minutes to finish your meal. Anybody not on their way out the door by then will be arrested and charged with criminal trespass!"

"I got a ulcer, my doctor tells me not to rush my food!" called out one worker, raising laughter and foot stomping around the world.

"I got sugar diabetes, I got to eat everything on my plate or my sugar drops and I'll pass out right here on the floor!" another said.

The police lieutenant pointed at the clock on the wall. Fifteen minutes! After that, you better be moving or you'll have a free ride to the Round House!"

Stella, Gloria and Moose leaned in to Lenny, asking what he thought they should do. "We have to consider how far we can push this, a lot of our retirees have disabilities. I don't think we should subject them to an arrest."

Stella agreed it would be asking a lot, but she felt they

were angry and determined enough to go the distance. "They know they're fighting for their survival, Lenny. A few hours in a cell isn't going to break their spirit, they're made of stronger stuff than that."

Lenny looked around the room at his coworkers. He had never been more proud of them than he was at that moment. He felt an urge to protect them from an uncomfortable experience; one possibly dangerous to the health of some of them. But at the same time he understood their long term needs were greater than the suffering a day's stay in a city jail could bring them.

He stood up, addressed the crowd. "It's up to all of you! Do we stay or do we go? What say you?"

"STAY! STAY! STAY!" the demonstrators chanted in unison. They banged their fists on the table and stomped their feet. They hooted and hollered. Tillie stood up and called on the Lord to bless their union and their struggle for a good life, raising cries of "Amen!"

Seeing the resistance of the demonstrators growing, West signaled to his sergeant, who tapped two officers on the arm and led them into the crowd. The security guard pointed at Lenny. Lenny looked at his nemesis West, wishing he could land a few good punches before the police had the handcuffs on him. But Lenny knew starting a fight would make things infinitely worse for him and for the union in court. He extended his arms for the handcuffs he knew were coming.

"Behind your back, Moss," said the security guard.

Lenny slowly turned around and allowed the police to place his wrists in the handcuffs. Although they were tight enough to threaten the circulation in his hands, he didn't grimace or betray the pain.

Moose was about to step forward when two more cops grabbed him and turned him around. Swearing loudly,

Moose called them every curse he could think of.

The demonstrators began to chant, "LET THEM GO! LET THEM GO!" They chanted even louder when the police arrested Gloria and Stella.

"Get them out of here!" the lieutenant ordered.

The police marched the four out into the hall and down toward the lobby. The entire crowd in the cafeteria followed them, continuing to chant. One retiree raised her cane and banged on the wall as they went. Startled visitors in the hallway stepped back, shocked at the scene, while several workers recorded it on their cell phones.

Reaching the main entrance, the officers led Lenny, Moose, Stella and Gloria down the broad marble steps toward a waiting police van. When the demonstrators on the sidewalk saw what was happening, they rushed toward the four in handcuffs. But a line of cops in riot gear quickly formed a human wall between them.

Seeing the police lieutenant walking beside Joe West, Patience rushed up to him. "What are you arresting them for?" she cried.

"Inciting a riot, to start with," said West. "And I'll arrest you, too, if you don't get off hospital property."

"Go ahead, arrest me, see if I care, you bastard!"

Birdie came up and took Patience by the arm. "Baby, we got to stay out of jail so we can raise their bail money, you know that. You can do more for him that way, you know they don't put men and women in the same cell."

"I know," said Patience, walking back to rejoin the demonstrators on the sidewalk, whose numbers had increased as workers from the hospital, out patients coming from appointments and visitors joined the protest. In her heart she yearned to be with her husband and the other arrested workers. But she realized they needed her on the outside raising money. And raising hell.

Malcolm took his mother's hand. He looked up at her, a worried expression on his face. "They ain't gonna beat on him, are they?" he asked.

"They aren't going to beat on him you mean. And no, they won't, there are too many of us watching him, he'll be fine."

Malcolm raised a fist in salute. Seeing the boy, Lenny winked at him, a proud smile on his face.

Patience called the union VP on her cell phone to inform him of what had happened. The union official told her he was already viewing the scenes from the cafeteria on his computer. "It's the police who incited the riot," he said. "That's clear from the videos." He promised to text her the name and phone number of a criminal defense lawyer, who would negotiate the bail. She and the others needed to raise bail money.

"Won't you be posting their bail?" she asked.

"It's better if you and the members raise it. Remember, this was supposed to be a spontaneous demonstration that the union didn't sanction." When Patience complained that raising money would take a lot of time and delay getting them out, the VP reminded her that going to the base to solicit support helped build union solidarity and would spread the word farther than if the union wrote a check and released a statement to the press. "It's what Lenny would do if he was on the outside."

In the end, Patience agreed to begin raising bail money. She and Birdie and other members went through the crowd explaining what they needed. They collected some money, with everyone promising they would go home and get more to bring to Lenny's house. A handful of union members agreed to stay on the picket line in front of the hospital until the four were released, while the rest used their bus tokens to go home, call all their friends and family, and raise money for bail.

On the bus ride back to their neighborhood, Malcolm asked his mother when Lenny would be out of jail. She explained that first they needed to raise money to pay to get him out. Hearing this, Malcolm asked if he could break his piggy bank so he could help get Lenny out of jail. Patience kissed his cheek. "Of course you can. Lenny will be proud when he hears what you've done."

31

Anna and Maribel were waiting for the bus from Florida to arrive on Filbert Street, just down from the Reading Terminal Market. "Is that the bus?" Maribel asked, growing excited every time a bus rolled down the street toward them.

"No, that bus is from Boston," said Anna. "You can see the name on the front of the bus. Look!" She pointed at the name displayed above the front windshield. "Mama's bus is coming from Washington, DC. That is where she changed buses."

"Oh, okay." Maribel took her backpack off her shoulder, unzipped it and sniffed inside it. "I hope she will like the cakes we made for her, they have the golden raisins and figs, just like she makes for us."

"It is the butter that makes them so good," said Anna, bending down to confirm the cakes were good enough to give to her mother. "Mama always used a lot of butter, never margarine."

Two more buses pulled up to the station and released their passengers. Maribel felt her stomach grumble. Anna had not let her eat any of the cakes they baked that morning; they were going to save them for when grandmother arrived and give her all of them. That way, Cecilia could share the cakes with them.

Finally a bus that said WASHINGTON came down the street toward them. Maribel pointed at the bus, shouting, "She's here! She's here!" She rushed up as soon as the bus came to a stop and stood beside the door.

With a loud whoosh the door opened. Passengers began to file out, looking sleepy and tired. Maribel hoped her grandmother had been able to sleep on the ride, she knew it took a whole day and a night for the bus to come from Florida, it was a very long way away.

Almost the last to emerge, Cecilia came down the steps of the bus, saw Maribel and Anna, and threw her arms out wide. "Ay, Maribel! Como estas? How is my little one?"

Maribel rushed to Cecelia and wrapped her arms around her.

"You are getting so big," said her grandmother.

"Mamá," said Anna. "You have only one little bag. Are you not going to stay very long with us?"

Cecilia answered she had simple needs, she was not going out. "All I need is one good dress for going to church. Otherwise my jeans are just fine."

"Grandma, we made cakes for you!" said Maribel.

"Good, I am hungry, hungry. When we get home we will have cakes and coffee, and hot chocolate for you!"

When she arrived at home from the demonstration, Patience began calling friends, relatives and coworkers to tell them about the arrests at the hospital and that they needed to raise bail money. She didn't yet know how much they would need, but she was sure it would be a substantial amount. "The hospital's going to claim all sorts of bullshit about what happened," she told a worker in radiology. "They'll make up shit about disrupting the working of the hospital and that sort of thing."

While on one call she saw another one coming in from Damien, Lenny's friend in the hospital IT department. She clicked over.

"Hey, Patience, I saw some of the videos from the demonstration. Wish I could have been there."

"Yeah, I know. Maybe one day you'll be in the union, too."

Damien suggested he set up a Facebook page for the demonstrators who were arrested. That way they could organize everyone's videos and photos in one place.

"Great idea, can you do that?"

"Actually, I already started, I figured Lenny wouldn't mind."

"Of course he wouldn't, thanks so much Damien." About to hang up, she added, "I know you've put your job on the line for him and all, but do you think you could contribute to the bail fund?"

"I started working on that, too," he said. Asked what he meant, Damien explained he'd begun building a crowd-sourcing fund raiser. Once it went live, everyone involved could share it with their friends and contacts. "We should raise a fair amount of money that way."

"We don't even know how much we need," said Patience.

"True, but beside bail money you'll need money for lawyers for the criminal trial. And if anyone is fired, they'll need financial support until they get reinstated, so..."

Patience could not believe how much Damien and the others were doing, taking initiative and helping defend the four workers in jail. Finding her emotion rising in her chest, making it hard to talk, she whispered good-bye and went out to sit in the back yard, trying to stay calm and plan for what was coming next.

<><><>

The ID Fellow carried a cup of hot tea into the ICU and brought it to Mr. Manwatty's bedside. "Here you are, my friend," said the Fellow. "I know you like tea with lemon and sugar, yes?"

Manwatty reached for the bed control and pressed the button, raising the head of the bed. "Thank you, doctor, that is very kind of you. I hope it was not very much trouble for you."

"Not at all. Although there was some kind of disturbance in the cafeteria. It seems several of the hospital workers are upset with the administration." With a satisfied smile on his lips, the Fellow told Manwatty that the microbiology lab had confirmed Dr. Augenello's diagnosis.

"Then I do have tuberculosis?"

"Yes. Unfortunately, you do not have it in your lungs, you have it in many of your other organs. It is a serious form of TB."

Manwatty sipped his tea and considered the information. He knew from how sick he felt that the illness was a bad one. But he had not understood it could easily have killed him.

"I am a lucky person to have such excellent doctors caring for me, am I not?"

"You are, indeed," said the Fellow, not wanting to alarm him with the statistics his boss had quoted just a few short days ago: that disseminated TB is almost always diagnosed in the autopsy suite.

The Fellow noted with satisfaction that the nurse had been able to discontinue the adrenalin infusion that had been needed to maintain the patient's blood pressure. "Your vital signs are improving. So are your lab results, all the trends are for the good."

"I do think I feel a little better. I still feel very weak, though. And I do not have much appetite."

"That's to be expected. As your body clears the infection, your strength and your appetite will continue to improve."

The Fellow got up to go when Manwatty said, "Oh, doctor, I forgot to tell you, I have heard from my mother in India. She says I did not receive the vaccination for TB that you asked me about."

The Fellow thanked him and left. At the nursing station where he updated the physician's progress notes in the computer, he considered how Mr. Manwatty's clinical course might have gone if the Hospitalist Service had followed Dr. Slocum's warnings and discontinued the TB drugs. By now the patient would be loaded onto the morgue cart and his body taken away for autopsy.

Not that Dr. Auginello would ever gloat or hold the victory over the Chief Medical Officer, that wasn't his way. Still, the Fellow wished that somebody would recognize what their team had done.

32

Standing at the bars of his jail cell, Lenny was annoyed that he had no way of knowing how Stella was doing, the officers working in the Round House wouldn't give him any information about other prisoners. Stella was tough and smart, he knew, but the retiree also had some serious health problems. He and Patience had driven Stella to more than one of her doctor's visits, so they knew about her diabetes and her heart disease.

"They shouldn't have taken Stella," Lenny grumbled to Moose. "Gloria, okay, she's young and healthy, but Stella's got a lot of medical problems."

"They shouldn't have arrested any of us," said Moose, sitting on the cement slab substituting for a bench.

"Tell me about it." Lenny paced up and down the jail cell. He'd made a call to Patience, who assured him they were raising bail money. He expected to go before the arraignment judge that evening, although he knew the court could postpone that until the following morning just to jerk his chain, they held all the cards.

"You think the union'll kick in for the bail money?" asked Moose.

"I doubt it, at least, not up front. We were supposed to be an unsanctioned action, remember? If they pay our bail, Croesus will argue that we were acting for the union, it will help them get out of our contract."

"They're slick bastards, ain't no doubt about it." He wondered aloud how high the bail was going to be.

"The hospital will try to get the District Attorney to argue for a high bail, you can count on that. They'll make up some bullshit about how we were interfering with the operation of the facility."

"That's crap, we were in the administrative wing. They got nothin' to do with running the hospital. Besides, it was Saturday, nobody was even there."

"Logic has nothing to do with their reasoning," said Lenny. "The cafeteria is part of the day to day operation. They'll probably claim we were inciting a riot. Calling for a walkout or some other disruption. It's a lie, but telling lies has never stopped them before."

"We had lots of workers taking videos. We could use them to show we weren't doing anything to interfere with patient care."

Lenny agreed, the videos would help their lawyer argue their case. "I wish I had my cell phone and could send some text messages, we could ask for those videos in court."

"No big deal," said Moose. "We'll have all that stuff ready when we go on trial. That's where it'll really matter."

"I guess you're right," said Lenny. "Nothing for us to do now but wait."

With time on his hands and no internet connection to put him in touch with his co-workers, Lenny finally had time to think about the investigation of Landry's death. He went over the facts that he knew so far with Moose, who reminded him that Anna Louisa was in worse legal trouble than they would ever be.

"I know, Mimi told me Miss Burgess would report Anna to the licensing board and they would pull her license. Even if she stays out of jail, it'll be hard for her to get work."

"Didn't that detective come up with anything to help her?"

"No, nothing. He didn't find anything in Landry's background that would explain why he was killed."

"No drugs or sex crimes?" asked Moose.

"Nope. He led a clean life as far as the police could find out."

"They just didn't dig deep enough."

"You're probably right," said Lenny. "If I could just figure out how he went into rigor mortis so quickly, that would at least answer one of the damned mysteries."

Lenny went over Anna's account of her night: how she'd made her hourly rounds, saw that Mr. Landry was breathing normally a little after six am, although she didn't take his blood pressure or pulse or given him any medication.

How could he be dead in bed and Anna not see that? How could she miss that for her five am rounds as well? Maybe even her four o'clock rounds?

It was baffling. And annoying.

"I've got a headache," said Lenny.

"Heh, heh. You need to go for a nice long run with me down Fairmont Park. Clear your head."

"I hate to admit it, but I'd be happy to go jogging with you if it would get me out of this damn place."

Lenny grasped the bars of the cell and looked out into the hall, wondering when the lawyer would arrive. And when he and Moose would go before the judge so they could get home and organize the fight that was coming.

<><><>

After dinner of a white bread sandwich with a thick slab of cheese, a bruised apple and a carton of skim milk, Lenny settled back and collected his thoughts. "I wish I had some paper and a pen, we need to put together plans for the campaign. We have to raise money for court costs. And we should meet with the union leadership, find out how much they were willing to do to help."

"Patience and Birdie and the rest are already on it, you can count on that," said Moose.

"Of course they are. I just can't stand being cut off and not being in the middle of it all."

"You mean, you hate not taking the lead on this."

Lenny hesitated. Though he knew there was a grain of truth in what Moose said, he felt he had always encouraged the rank and file to take leadership roles in every campaign. "I don't know, Moose. I mean, it's not like I try to make every decision. Or insist everything go my way all the time. I do listen to every suggestion, even if it's crazy or unrealistic."

"Yeah, you a good listener. But you have strong opinions, and you don't hold back saying them. You got years of experience leading the union, people respect that. Sometimes they keep quiet 'cause they know you got the experience and all."

"Hmm. So it sounds like you're saying my being in jail for a day and a night is a good thing, as far as leading the fight."

Moose told his friend sometimes a bad break for one was a good break for somebody else.

Lenny was mulling over Moose's words, trying not to deny their validity, when a guard approached their cell accompanied by a man carrying an old leather attaché case. The guard let the man into the cell, then locked it behind him.

"Mister Moss?" the man said, holding his hand out to Lenny. "I am Manuel Oliveras. I'm here to represent you and Mister Maddox and the two ladies who were arrested with you." He shook Moose's hand in turn. "You fellows all right in here?"

"We're all right," said Moose. "What's happening outside?"

Regis told them there was a committee set up to raise bail money, they would have several thousand dollars by the time their case went before the judge for arraignment.

"Did the union put any money in the pot?" asked Moose.

"They have not. So far. The union believes it would undermine their argument that your demonstration was conducted spontaneously, and not under the president's leadership." Seeing the disappointment on Moose's face, the lawyer added that the union was going to make their auditorium available for fund raising, and they were already reaching out to the membership to contribute to the defense fund.

"Apparently somebody has already set up a crowd sourced web site where people can make contributions," said Oliveras. Lenny had a good idea it was his friend Damien in the IT department.

"How high you think the bail's gonna be?" asked Moose.

"The hospital's gonna lean on the city, try to get it set high."

"They'll probably claim we were inciting a riot," Lenny added. "That we were disrupting the operation of the hospital."

"Yes, I'm anticipating an argument about the bail on those grounds. Lucky for us, there are already several videos from the incident in the cafeteria. One of your co-workers has set up a Facebook page and posted them. I've looked them over, and they clearly show you were not preventing other workers from buying lunch or going back to work."

"You saw the cops in riot gear?" said Lenny. "That was totally unnecessary."

"I agree, and I will argue as such in court."

Asked if they would likely have enough money that night to be released, Oliveras told them there was no way to predict the amount, but he thought they would likely make bail and be released that night.

"I will be in court when you are called up, leave everything to me. And don't say anything. Not to the district attorney, not to the judge."

"We know the drill, I've told people myself," said Lenny. "Nobody talks, everyone walks."

"Exactly." Oliveras shook their hands and signaled to be released, while Lenny and Moose settled back to wait, to worry, and to remember.

33

As they were escorted into the court room, Moose took one look at the judge, a florid faced, pudgy man with reddish brown hair and a frowning mouth, and whispered to Lenny, "Damn. Looks like we got a red neck for a judge."

Lenny jabbed Moose with his elbow, signaling to keep quiet. He was glad to see that Stella appeared to be in good health and good spirits. The retiree had walked into the courtroom ahead of him with shoulders back, head high, leaning on her cane a bit more than was usual, no doubt to try and gain sympathy from the judge. Gloria walked beside her, looking pissed off.

Casting his eyes about the room, he spotted Patience in the back, who gave him a furtive waive. Birdie beside her looked worried. One of the union VPs was beside them, a reassuring sight, it meant they were actively supporting the defense.

Manuel Oliveras sat at the defense table as the four accused stood before the judge. He waited as the assistant district attorney read the charges, which included criminal trespass, inciting a riot, resisting arrest and criminal mischief. "Your honor, in light of the severity and the violence of these criminal acts, I ask that the bail be set at one millions dollars for each suspect."

As the defense attorney Oliveras rose to object, the district attorney added, "I have the chief of their Security Department, Mister Joseph West, here to offer testimony if your honor wishes to hear an account of the incidents."

The judge turned to the defense attorney, who had remained standing. "Your honor, to begin with, the charge of criminal trespass is entirely without foundation. The hospital cafeteria is open to the public. You cannot charge someone with trespass when there are no barriers to entering the establishment."

"The cafeteria was closed during the demonstration," the District Attorney countered. "The demonstrators were given an order to disperse after the closing of the cafeteria. They refused and were subsequently arrested."

"Untrue and misleading, your honor. The cafeteria was only closed to give the police an excuse to arrest hospital employees and retirees who were exercising their constitutional rights of assembly and free speech. What's more, they were given a fifteen minute grace period before having to vacate the premises, but the police arrested them immediately after that announcement."

"That does not obviate the charges of inciting a riot and of criminal mischief. Public or private, their behavior was interfering with the hospital's provision of services."

Oliveras argued that if anyone had incited a riot, it was the James Madison security department, which called in a swat team in full riot gear. "This excessive show of force was unnecessary and inflammatory. It was the police, with their truncheons and face shields and body armor that raised the level of emotion in the room!"

"There's no need for speeches, Mister Oliveras, just stick to the facts," said the judge.

"Yes, your honor. Three of the defendants are hard-working hospital employees with impeccable records, the forth is a retiree who is in poor health and clearly could not pose a threat to public safety. They were only distributing information about the hospital administration's threat to withdraw support for their health benefits and pensions."

"Not true!" said the District Attorney. "They openly called on the employees in the cafeteria to abandon their work stations and join them in the protest. That was disruptive to the provision of care that James Madison was established to provide."

"If it please the court." Oliveras asked if he could approach the bench. With a nod of assent from the judge, he and the District Attorney stepped cautiously up to the judge's desk.

Taking out his cell phone, Oliversas said, "Your honor, some of the hospital employees taking their lunch break at the time of the demonstration recorded the events on their cell phones. The videos have been collected on a web site by another employee. I invite your honor to view any of the videos. You will clearly see that it was the police in riot gear that inflamed the people in the cafeteria, and that the demonstrators never called on those who were at work to abandon their posts."

The District Attorney objected, claiming the court had no way to verify the authenticity of the videos, but the judge waived him off. "This is just an arraignment for bail, you can object when it goes to trial."

Taking the cell phone from the defense attorney, the judge played one of the videos. The sounds of the demonstrators could be heard on the little speaker, as could the orders from the police lieutenant to vacate the cafeteria immediately.

"You will see that the police in riot gear have closed off the two exits and are preventing people from leaving. They are the ones keeping employees from returning to their work stations, not my clients."

With his mouth open to object, the DA was silenced by a motion of the judge's hand. He played a second video. "I can see they were marching up and down in the middle of the room, but nobody appears to be prevented from taking their lunch." Looking directly at the District Attorney, he added, "I don't hear any demonstrators urging employees on the clock to abandon their post."

Oliveras pointed to the scene of Lenny being arrested. "Your honor will note, my client in no way resisted arrest. He went willingly without protest or struggle."

Agreeing that the videos clearly supported the defense attorney's arguments, the judge handed the phone back to Oliveras. He ordered bail set at ten thousand dollars each, cash or bond.

As Lenny was led out of the court room, he looked back at Patience, who held up a hand with three fingers raise. He knew that meant they had three thousand dollars on hand. He estimated they could raise the last thousand dollars by the following afternoon.

Moose was downhearted as the police locked him and Lenny back in their cell. "Forty-thousand dollars. Where we gonna raise that kind of money?"

Lenny told him not to worry. "We don't have to actually have that much in our hand. We go to a bail bondsman and put up ten per cent. He pays the whole thing, and we settle what we owe him when we show up for trial."

"So we only need four thousand?"

"Yup. Patience signaled me that they already had three. It shouldn't take too long to raise the rest. They'll probably have it by tomorrow afternoon."

"So which one of us is gonna be spending the night?"

Lenny offered to stay, but Moose shook his head. "I say we flip a coin," he said, taking a penny from his pocket.

"Okay," said Lenny. "Heads you win, tails I lose."

"Don't even try it." Moose called it heads and flipped the coin up into the air. It landed, bounced, spun a few times and settled onto the concrete floor.

It came up tails.

"Shit," said Moose. "I can't take this prison food any-more."

"Tell you what. I'll hang out here with you until they raise the last thousand and we'll go out together. Okay?"

"That's crazy and you know it," said Moose. "Ain't no need for you to stay in this damn jail."

"You're right, there's no need, it's something I want to do. You'd do it for me if I lost the coin toss!"

"No fricking way. Get your ass out of here, I'll see you in a few."

34

Riding home a little after midnight, Patience sat in the back seat with Lenny while Moose sat in the front with Birdie, who was driving. "I'm so glad we got Stella and Gloria out," said Patience. "I was worried she would be stuck in that cold cell all night long. With her diabetes and heart trouble and god knows what else..."

"The judge shouldn't have made her have to put up bail money," said Moose. "Woman like her, don't make no sense."

"I know you signaled me you had the three thousand dollars," said Lenny. "Where did you get the last thousand with the banks closed and all?"

"Actually, when you were standing in front of the judge we had three and a half," said Birdie. "We only needed five hundred more. Your union president sent the money by messenger."

"Really? Five hundred?"

"Yup. Five hundred, cash. We're not supposed to let on where it came from."

Pulling up to Lenny's house, Patience asked if Birdie and Moose wanted to come in for something to eat. Their children were with relatives, so there was no urgency to go straight home.

"I don't know 'bout you," said Moose, "but I could use a drink."

"I agree. Forget about food, we have a bottle of bourbon that's been waiting to give itself up for a good cause, and this is it."

At home Patience sent the neighbor who had been watching the children home with thanks while Lenny brought out the liquor, ice, and for his wife, ginger ale.

"She doesn't really like the taste of whiskey," he said, pouring Patience a short shot mixed with soda and over ice. "I'll take mine neat."

Once settled in the living room, Lenny asked if anyone had heard from Anna Louisa, the police having taken his cell phone, so he couldn't receive any calls or messages while in custody. Neither Patience nor Birdie had heard any news about the nurse.

"I had some time to think about the case. I knew Anna was going to be charged, so I could imagine how devastating it would be for her to be locked up like we were. Only her charges were serious, they weren't going to offer her any bail."

"What did you figure out?" asked Birdie.

"Not a damn thing. All that dead time didn't do me any good. I still can't understand why anyone would intentionally kill Mister Landry. I mean, Detective Williams tells me the background check didn't come up with any criminal or suspicious behavior."

"What makes you think the murder was all about Mister Landry?" asked Patience, sipping her bourbon and soda.

"How's that?" said Lenny, a single dark eyebrow raised in surprise.

"Well, if there was no particular reason to kill Mister Landry, maybe he was just in the wrong place at the wrong time."

"You mean, an accidental death? Someone gave the insulin to the wrong patient by mistake?"

"I suppose so," said Patience. "Or then again, maybe not."

"Oh, I see where you're going," said Birdie. "You think somebody could have murdered Landry, but not because he was Mister Landry. They killed him for some other reason."

"Yes, that's what I mean."

Lenny held his glass up to his mouth and took a drink. He let the bourbon swirl around in his mouth, enjoying the flavor and the warmth it gave him. "So you're saying, maybe the killer gave Landry the fatal insulin injection intentionally, but not because he was Landry, but because... because why?"

They all looked at each other, lost in thought and unable to think of a reason to kill whoever was in the bed that Landry happened to have occupied that fatal night.

"Wait a second," said Moose. "Somebody kills a patient in a hospital bed. Why? What do they get for it?"

"Well if it's the usual kind of serial killer that operates in hospitals and nursing home, it's to bring the patient back to life and earn all kinds of praise."

"To look like the hero," said Birdie.

"Yes. But this doesn't fit that pattern. Anna didn't rush in and try to revive the patient, she left him in bed, dead and stiff. He was found on the next shift."

"Okay," said Birdie. "But who would benefit from Mister Landry dying? Did he leave a big life insurance for his wife? An inheritance? Something like that?"

"No," said Lenny, "the detective said he didn't even have a life insurance policy. And his estate didn't amount to anything. Not enough to kill him for it, that's for sure."

He freshened everyone's drink, surprised that Patience accepted a second. She swirled the ice cubes in her drink with her finger, then licked the whiskey and soda from her finger.

"What if killing Landry got somebody something important? Like, say, a promotion at work."

"Sure," said Birdie. "What if another man had the hots for his wife? He killed Landry to get at her."

"He wasn't married."

More sipping, less talking as they all pondered the problem. Then Lenny put down his glass and took out his cell phone. "Of course! I am such an incredible ass!" he said, scrolling through the address book for a phone number.

"What do you mean?" said Patience

"Wait a second, I have to call Seven-South, it's too late to call Mimi."

Lenny waited several rings before someone picked up the phone. "Hi, Maddy, is that you? It's Lenny...Yes, I'm out of jail, thank you for asking. Listen, I need to know something about the night Mister Landry died. The B bed by the window was empty, right?"

Lenny nodded his head vigorously, letting his friends know the answer to his question was a yes.

"And, now this is really, really important, was the curtain between the beds drawn when they coded Landry?"

Lenny waited while Maddy tried to recall exactly how the room looked at the time of the arrest. The others in the room leaned forward, eager to know where Lenny was going with his line of questions.

"The curtain was drawn," Lenny repeated Maddy's words."All night long. Gotcha." He explained to his friends and wife that the night staff kept a curtain drawn across an empty bed so the night supervisor wouldn't see it was empty and try to find them an admission.

"Thank you very much for answering my questions, Maddy, you have been extremely helpful. Have a good shift."

Closing his phone, Lenny picked up his drink and took a sip, then he opened the phone again and made another call. After several rings, a groggy voice answered.

"Hello, Anna Louisa? It's Lenny. I'm so sorry to wake you, but I need to know something. Are you awake enough to talk?"

After a pause, Lenny said, "Okay, so you told me the night that Mister Landry died, you didn't see his face because he was turned away from the door. Is that right?" Lenny nodded his head as the others watched him.

"I see," said Lenny. "You didn't get a look at his face, it was hidden by the pillow. Okay, thanks. I'm sorry to wake you, but it was important I get it right. Try not to worry, I'll explain everything to you when I see you tomorrow. Good-night."

He hung up the phone, picked his drink back up and rolled some of the whiskey around in his mouth, enjoying the silence in the room as he held everyone in suspense.

Finally Patience blurted out, "Tell me what you're thinking, Lenny, or I'll kill you right here in front of everybody!"

"You were right," he said. "Whoever killed Landry didn't do it to hurt *Landry*, it was to hurt the person responsible for his health."

"His nurse!" said Patience.

"Yes. Anna Louisa."

Moose agreed, the killer must have wanted to get Anna fired and have her license revoked. And to get her charged with murder. "You know there's only one person who'd want that to happen."

"Yes,' said Lenny. "Only one person stands to gain. Her ex-husband, Jimmy. He wants custody of their daughter. This was the only way he was going to get it."

Lenny's phone softly hummed as he called Detective Williams. He thought it would go to voice message, but after the third ring he heard a sleepy voice croak, "What, Moss?"

"I know who killed Landry. You want to hear the name?"

Lenny held his empty glass up high for a toast as he said the name, "Jimmy Cruz. Former husband of Anna Louisa Rodriguez and all around piece of crap. He killed Landry knowing the hospital would blame the nurse and he would end up getting custody of their daughter. Cruz was in the A-bed pretending to be the patient, the dead man was in the B bed behind the curtain." Lenny heard the detective groan as the inexorable logic of Lenny's words sank in.

He went on to explain that the killer had his face turned away from the door, and he was partially concealed by the pillow. He used to work as a salesman...for a drug company, so he probably kept the ID badge that would get him into the hospital.

When the detective agreed to pick up the suspect for questioning, Lenny told him, "Look on the bright side, you can take all the credit for the arrest, I don't need the honors."

Hanging up the phone, Lenny held up his glass and made the toast: "To Anna and daughter, and to happy endings!"

35

The following morning, when Lenny called to tell Anna Louise the police had arrested Jimmy, she broke down and cried. He went on to say the police had found good criminal evidence against Jimmy: the lot number of the insulin syringe in Mister Landry's medication bin was traced to a friend of Jimmy who was a diabetic and admitted selling him the insulin. The police found hospital scrubs in his apartment, insulin syringes, and a fake James Madison ID badge as well.

"Maybe he copied my ID when he was still visiting Maribel and substituted his name and picture," said Anna. "That was when everything turned bad."

"You're probably right," said Lenny. "Oh, what did they fire him for?"

"He was stealing drug samples he was supposed to give to the doctors."

"Well, the detective told me the case against him is strong, I expect he'll be gone from your life for a long time. And from Maribel's, too."

"Lenny, I can't thank you enough! Not in a million years I can't! I will go to church with my mother and my daughter and say a prayer for you and Mimi and everyone who helped me."

"I'm just glad things will work out for you. When do you have your hearing before the licensing board?"

"It is supposed to be next week. But I had a call from Human Resources this morning. They think Miss Burgess will let me come back, so maybe there will be no hearing."

"That's wonderful news, Anna, I'm very, very happy for you. Let me know what goes down, and hopefully I will see you at shift change soon. Bye."

Lenny looked at his watch. It was almost one pm, Sunday afternoon. He was exhausted and exhilarated at the same time, like a drunk wired on too much coffee. What to do — call Stella and Gloria and see how they were doing, or turn off his phone and take a long nap? He knew he couldn't call Moose, his friend would insist he go out jogging in Fairmont Park. Lenny felt he hadn't energy enough to climb the stairs and get back into bed.

But sleep was singing its siren song to him. He trudged upstairs, pulling off his shirt as he reached the landing. When he opened the door to the bedroom, he saw that Patience had stripped the bed and taken the sheets down to the basement to be laundered.

"I...don't...give a shit," he mumbled to himself. Kicking off his shoes, he wrapped himself in the comforter and laid his weary head down on the bare pillow. His last thought was how Patience would react when she came upstairs with the laundry and saw him sleeping on the bare mattress. He wished he could see her while he was sleeping, it would almost be worth waking up for.

Mr. Manwatty was grinning like an infant who had his favorite food in his hand and all over his face as the orderly pushed his wheelchair down the Seven-South hallway. He was out of the intensive care unit and back on the regular ward. No more high pressure oxygen masks forcing air down into his lungs. No more heart monitors ringing, ringing, ringing all night long whenever he turned over or scratched his chest.

The nurse who helped settle him into bed asked if he was hungry, she already had diet orders for him.

"Yes, please, nurse, I am most hungry. I feel I could eat enough for three men!"

"I'll put in for double portions, then," she said, entering the diet request into her portable computer. "Is there anything else I can get you?"

Manwatty looked around the room, thinking there was nothing more he needed now that the death sentence of the TB infection had been lifted. Now that he was back among the living.

"I wonder, nurse, if it is not too much trouble, if you could give me a few sheets of paper and a few envelopes. I want to thank the doctors for their excellent care."

The nurse left to collect paper and pen, while Manwatty stretched out on his bed, raised the head of the bed so that it was at just the right angle to be comfortable. He introduced himself to his roommate, a middle aged man in bright red pajamas.

"Those are most handsome pajamas you are wearing," Manwatty said. "They let you not have to wear the hospital gown?"

The gentleman winked. "I had my wife bring in a dozen donuts. You treat the nurses good, they'll let you do anything."

"That is good to know," said Manwatty, vowing to be sure and write a letter to the director of nursing praising the care. Especially nurse Gary Tuttle, who identified the incorrect color of his urine and quite likely saved his life.

<><><>

After folding the clean laundry and piling it neatly in the laundry basket, Patience was coming up the stairs when the phone rang. It was the vice president of the Hospital Service Workers Union asking to speak with Lenny.

"I think he went upstairs, let me go check," she said.

Climbing the stairs, she opened the bedroom door and was about to call her husband's name when she saw him curled up in the comforter, fast asleep. Smiling at the sight of her love in his slumber, she silently closed the door and went back downstairs to the phone.

"I'm sorry, Lenny's taking a long overdue nap. Can I take a message for him?"

"Oh, of course. Just tell him James Madison has withdrawn its threat to divest itself from the benefits and welfare fund, at least for now. That doesn't mean they won't try it again down the road, but at least for the rest of this year, our benefits should be safe."

"Okay, I'll tell him when he wakes up, thanks so much for the good news. Bye!"

She looked at the laundry basket, then at the clock on a table. It was early, there was a State Store open on Sunday. She decided to go out and buy a bottle of really good bourbon for Lenny to celebrate.

"Kids!" she called to Malcolm and Takia. "Want to go to the store with me? We can bring home pizza!"

36

On Monday morning Evie was bringing a cart of fresh linen to dialysis unit when she saw Joe West walking toward her. Feeling her throat tighten with fear, Evie resolved to address the man, despite her anxiety. After all, she had kept her end of the bargain, reporting to him everything she heard about the union's plans. She was owed, fair is fair.

"Mister West?" she said, her mouth dry.

West came to an abrupt halt. "What is it?" he snapped.

"I haven't heard nothin' about me getting into the dialysis training. I was just wondering—"

"You failed the math exam," he said. "And your English comprehension was just as bad. You can't work in an occupation that you don't have the basic skills to master."

"But you promised."

"Stick with the laundry, it's where you belong," he said and continued on his way, leaving Evie broken hearted. She pushed her cart into the dialysis unit and stood a moment staring at the techs and nurses. They were all busy giving the treatments, writing in the charts and chatting happily with the patients. It was a world she would never know; a life she would never lead.

With a heavy sigh she began piling the fresh sheets onto the closet shelves, wishing she never had anything to do with that devil Joe West.

<><><>

Dr. Michael Auginello walked alongside his ID Fellow down the center aisle of the hospital auditorium. Auginello was looking forward to hear the guest speaker for this week's Medical Grand Rounds talk about new therapeutic approaches to multi-drug resistant TB.

As he walked past the first few rows, a doctor who was past the usual retirement age but still hale and hearty spied Auginello. He nodded to Auginello and began to clap his hands. Several of the other physicians, physician assistants, students and nurses turned to see what the senior physician was clapping about. Realizing it was for Dr. Auginello, they immediately joined in.

Dr. Fahim, the ICU attending, was seated by the aisle. Fahim stood up while applauding. In seconds the entire room was on their feet clapping their hands.

Perplexed, Auginello stepped over to Fahim and said, "Samir, what the hell is this about?"

Fahim clapped his friend on the shoulder. "Michael, don't you understand? You won! You beat the machine!"

"Are you talking about Teepee?"

"Of course! You stuck to your diagnosis when the computer said you were wrong, and you beat it! It's wonderful. It restores our faith in the superiority of the physician and his team over some arrogant algorithm."

Still having trouble understanding why people would applaud him for simply doing his job as best he could, Auginello found a seat, along with his Fellow. Once he was sitting down, the others resumed their seats and the Chief Medical Officer, Dr. Slocum, introduced the guest speaker, not daring to address the applause and the issue that it raised.

The speaker called up the first slide of his presentation and was beginning to explain the difficulties involved in testing new compounds against a bacterium that was notoriously difficult to grow in the lab, when Auginello's cell phone beeped three times, indicating he had a page.

Opening the phone, the ID Attending saw a message from the Emergency Room. They had a possible meningitis case and needed his consultation STAT. The ER staff always freaked out when they suspected bacterial meningitis, since one of the bacterial species that infected the brain was highly transmissible and sometimes fatal.

He showed the message to his ID Fellow, who rose and went off to make an initial assessment, while Auginello settled back, stuck his long legs out into the aisle, and enjoyed hearing some good old fashioned medical science.

Seated in one of Birdie's battered old folding chairs sipping a cup of coffee, Lenny was listening to Moose talk about their time in jail, content to not say a word, while Regis Devoe laughed at every one of Moose's anecdotes.

"I knew we'd be out o' that cell before morning, Birdie and Patience and the rest were collecting for our bail money. It wasn't any big thing, but old Lenny was totally pissed off."

"That Joe West had no right, getting the police to bust you that way," said Birdie. "The videos on the internet showed the police were the problem, not you and the workers. I mean come on, all that riot gear the cops were wearing, they looked like storm troopers from some Star Wars movie."

235

Moose said, "The videos got like a million hits, the whole city knows there was no riot, we were just protesting their taking away our benefits. The cops were the problem, not us."

He looked at Lenny, who had kept quiet. "What's the matter, Lenny, cat got your tongue?"

The wily detective looked at his friend. "I was just thinking, our arrest was a big boost to the union campaign, it got everybody even more pissed off. The image of poor old Stella being led out of the hospital in handcuffs, walking with two cops holding her up..."

"Yeah, and one of them was even holding her cane!" said Birdie, chuckling at the image she'd watched on the video. "The hospital bosses sure looked like a bunch of fools."

Moose told them the union VP swore the city was going to drop the charges against them. The publicity of the trial would bring the videos back into the news. That would be even more damaging to the hospital's reputation.

"You were smart posting the video clips of the security guard recording you," said Regis. "That made the hospital look even stupider than at the demonstration."

"They quit following you around the hospital yet?" asked Birdie.

Lenny confirmed, for now Joe West had backed off dogging his movements, although he was sure in time West would find some new way to harass him.

Just then Mimi knocked and entered the sewing room, a smile on her face bright enough to light up the room.

"Hey, did you guys hear, they reinstated Anna Louisa! Isn't that wonderful?"

Everyone agreed, it was good news.

"She's using some of her vacation time to think about what she wants to do. I've got a feeling she's going to resign and look for another job. Can't say as I blame her,

236

Mother Burgess was a royal bitch, the way she reported Anna to the nursing board. She'll have Anna's work under a microscope, checking everything Anna does"

Lenny was puzzled. Seeing the GPS unit dangling from Mimi's neck, he pointed at it, indicating his concern that the nurse had spoken bluntly about the director of nursing.

Mimi laughed long and hard. "Oh, Lenny, it's so funny. The GPS doesn't receive down here in the sewing room. I found that out last week. Damien, one of the I-T guys told me, they don't have the antennas down here to pick up the signal, so I can say whatever the hell I want, the dispatcher won't hear me." She lifted the unit so it was close to her lips. *"Whatever the hell I want."*

Birdie threw back her head and laughed. "You got to invite your nursing friends to come down here for their breaks. Ain't nobody gonna bother us here."

Mimi asked if it was true, the police had good evidence against Jimmy for murdering Mr. Landry. Lenny confirmed, they found syringes and a fake hospital ID in his apartment. They were also reviewing security tapes from the hallway, there was a figure who resembled Jimmy seen going down the hall toward Landry's room.

"They could've found that on day one," said Birdie. Lenny agreed, once they had picked out Anna Louisa as the one who administered the insulin, the police made no effort to look for another suspect.

"The killer was slick, he gave the insulin in the patient's IV so it wouldn't wake him," said Regis. "You can't give a sleeping patient an injection, he'll jump out of his bed."

"Poor Mister Landry," said Mimi. "He was getting a last liter of IV fluid to flush his kidneys after his chemo. When Anna Louisa checked the room on her hourly rounds, it was Jimmy in the A bed pretending to be the patient, but he had already killed the patient and moved him to the B bed. That's how come I found him in full rigor."

"That's what happened," said Lenny.

"Now I get why Beatrice had to remake the B bed that morning, it wasn't neat and trim the way we make up a bed. I told that Detective Williams about it when he came back to ask me a second time about what happened the morning I called the code."

Lenny saw the time on the wall clock. "I better get back, break time's over."

"I'll go with you," said Mimi, opening the door.

"Oh, Moose, do me a favor, drop this off with Damien in IT for me? I owe him a bottle of bourbon." He handed a package to his friend, who promised not to sample the contents before taking it to Big D.

As Mimi stood in the open door, she paused for a second, looking at the sewing room, with Birdie at her big, black industrial sewing machine and Moose seated beside her. "You know something? I'm going to bring some of my nursing friends down here for break. We can say whatever we want and nobody's going to hear us. It's about time we all got together."

"They try to take away our benefits and pension today, they're gonna take away yours tomorrow," said Birdie.

"True that," said Mimi. "And the first issue we're gonna organize around is these damn GPS units. They have got to go. I want to pee in private, it's my god damned constitutional right!"

Lenny walked out with her, laughing harder than he'd laughed in a long time. He couldn't wait to get home and tell Malcolm and Takia the story about Mimi and the GPS units. Over pizza from Giovanni's, it was their favorite.

Made in the USA
Middletown, DE
29 April 2016